## "I still haven't made my point," she said.

Angus leaned forward, his hand touching the lace of her underwear now, his lips a breath away from hers. "And your point is?"

She'd forgotten. But she was damned if she was going to admit it.

"My point is that you're a bounder, a cad, an incorrigible flirt and a sensualist, with whom a lady cannot be safe."

"I object. I am not a bounder." His voice was even more English and upper-class than normal. "I have a suspicion you like it when I'm a cad, though."

He feathered his fingertips over the lace covering her sex, and Elisabeth gasped.

The cab stopped.

## THE ELIGIBLE BACHELORS

### *They're strong, sexy, seductive... and single!*

These gorgeous men are used to driving women wild—they've got the looks, the cash and that extra special something....

They're also resolutely commitment-free! But will these bachelors change their playboy ways after meeting our four feisty females?

Find out in this month's collection from Promotional Presents!

Available now:

*Wife for a Week*
Kelly Hunter

*Mistress on Trial*
Kate Hardy

*MacAllister's Baby*
Julie Cohen

*The Firefighter's Chosen Bride*
Trish Wylie

# MACALLISTER'S BABY

## JULIE COHEN

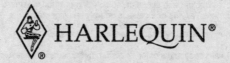

TORONTO • NEW YORK • LONDON
AMSTERDAM • PARIS • SYDNEY • HAMBURG
STOCKHOLM • ATHENS • TOKYO • MILAN • MADRID
PRAGUE • WARSAW • BUDAPEST • AUCKLAND

ISBN-13: 978-0-373-82055-9
ISBN-10: 0-373-82055-0

MacALLISTER'S BABY

First North American Publication 2007.

Previously published in the U.K. under the title *Delicious*.

This edition published by arrangement with Harlequin Books S.A.

® and TM are trademarks of the publisher. Trademarks indicated with ® are registered in the United States Patent and Trademark Office, the Canadian Trade Marks Office and in other countries.

www.eHarlequin.com

Printed in U.S.A.

# MACALLISTER'S
# BABY

For Stan.

# CHAPTER ONE

ELISABETH paused, listening, her knuckles hovering over the surface of the food technology classroom door.

Inside it was completely silent.

She checked her watch: ten-thirteen, midway through period three. She'd passed by here last week during her free period and it had been far from silent—downright noisy, in fact.

The silence disturbed Elisabeth more than any screams would have done. In theory, a silent classroom was A Good Thing. In real life, a silent classroom meant that the students inside were absorbed in something besides cooking.

Which was A Very Bad Thing.

'Please let there not be any blood or fire,' she muttered. She shoved the stack of reports she'd brought for Tasha Cutter to sign underneath her arm, leaned forward, and listened.

She heard the rustle and cough of children. The sound of a chair being scraped back. And softly, just at the limit of her hearing, a cluck.

A *cluck*?

Okay, this was weird. Elisabeth slowly opened the door.

The room was still. About thirty twelve-year-old students were sitting in a circle, their eyes fixed on the centre of the room. Some of them had their mouths open. She heard another cluck.

A man stood in the centre of the circle with his back to her. He was tall, dark-haired, wearing trousers tailored to his long legs, a midnight-blue shirt that fit his broad shoulders, and Elisabeth didn't recognise him. He certainly wasn't Tasha.

A strange man, in a teacherless classroom, clucking?

Maybe she should investigate, but, as odd as this man was, he seemed to have the children under control. He was standing motionless, his hands held out to his sides at shoulder height as if he were about to conduct an orchestra. From the doorway, looking at the backs of his hands, she could see they were strong and sculpted. The thumbs were well developed, the fingers long, the nails clean and blunt, even the veins somehow precise. They were hands that looked good at doing things, even now, as they were poised in the air, empty.

Elisabeth wanted to touch them.

The thought was so unexpected that she leaned a little harder on the doorknob. The door opened another inch. The hinges creaked. And then the room exploded.

Something shrieked, and a streak of white feathers flew across the floor, between the children's legs. The students jumped up, knocking over chairs, crying out.

'It's there!'

'Lookit that thing go!'

'Over there, get it!'

A boy she recognised as Jimmy Peto launched himself off a desk, arms outstretched to catch his feathered prey. A white, beaked, madly clucking thing flapped its wings and ran away from him, over Elisabeth's polished shoes. Its claws briefly stung the bare top of her foot before it was gone.

It was a chicken.

The bird wedged itself underneath one of the kitchen units. Immediately six children surrounded it, trying to poke at it with hands and wooden spoons taken from the utensil drawers. The chicken made a panicked sound and pecked at its tormentors.

It was only a matter of time before somebody lost an eye. Or discovered the knife drawer.

Elisabeth stepped into the room, opened her mouth, drew in a breath from her diaphragm.

'Get back. Now.'

She hadn't said it. It was a male voice, deep, gravelly, with cut-glass enunciation. The students who clustered around the chicken responded to the authority in the voice. They shuffled back, and then the chicken squawked again.

'Year seven,' Elisabeth ordered. 'Go back to your seats.'

'Who are you?'

The man was standing in front of her, facing her now. He was tall, and that was saying something, because Elisabeth was five feet ten and didn't often have to look up at people. He had grey eyes, a dimple in his chin, and he smelled like fresh lemons.

Attraction hit her like recognition, with a thump of her heart and a catch of her breath. She swallowed, mouth suddenly dry, world suddenly not making sense any more.

'It's Miss Read,' said little Jimmy Peto, who had given up chasing the chicken and now stood at Elisabeth's side. 'She teaches English.'

'Glad to meet you, Miss Read who teaches English.' The man's lips tilted up into a smile, and his grey eyes sparkled at her. 'I have things under control here, if you want to go back to your Shakespeare.'

Elisabeth swallowed again. No. She was *not* supposed to feel this way, as if she'd run a marathon while she'd stood here, her heart straining and her breath shallow, her legs trembling beneath her. Not supposed to feel this way ever, and certainly not because of a man.

She shook her head. *Remember where you are,* she told herself. *School. Your world. Everything makes sense here.*

'You've got thirty children, a roomful of dangerous equipment, and a live chicken on the loose,' Elisabeth said. 'I don't think this is under control, Mr—'

'MacAllister, miss,' Jimmy supplied.

'Mr MacAllister.' The name wasn't familiar; he wasn't a regular supply teacher at this school.

Talking like this, setting things in order, reasserting her world, made her feel more like herself. 'Perhaps you should fetch your chicken,' she said.

Her eyes met his grey ones again in a wordless challenge. She saw him raise his eyebrows, and his mouth quirked with humour.

'All right,' he said. And then he smiled, a broad, full-face, eye-twinkling smile.

Elisabeth's stomach turned to quicksilver. His smile transformed his face, lit up the entire room. It was blinding, brilliant, beautiful, and Elisabeth forgot the children, the chicken, the classroom, her own name.

She did recognise him.

With a swift movement, he covered the distance from the front of the classroom to the unit underneath which the chicken cowered. 'Come here, MacNugget,' he murmured, sweeping the bird out from under the unit and into his arms. In seconds it was shut away in a plastic animal carrier on one of the kitchen counters. He winked at her as he closed its door.

'Angus MacAllister?' she gasped.

He was no supply teacher.

'He's that chef off the TV, miss,' Jimmy told her. 'My mum watches him every Tuesday night. And my gran.'

Angus MacAllister. TV chef, celebrity cookbook author, owner of one of the most expensive and highly rated restaurants in London. She'd watched his programme a few times and noticed vaguely that he was attractive, in the way that everybody on television was attractive.

He looked different in reality. Much more...real.

And a million times sexier. She tried to breathe deeply to calm down, but she only smelled his scent, and that didn't help.

'What are you doing at the Slater School?' she asked. 'And why have you got a chicken?'

The students had all subsided. The chicken was out of sight in its box and these two adults sparring were more interesting than mayhem.

'Until you frightened MacNugget, I was using her to show these kids where their breakfast had come from.'

Elisabeth doubted many of the children in this room had had an egg for breakfast. Chances were that a lot of them didn't get breakfast very often, full stop.

Many of the Slater School's pupils came from low-income households, families where both parents had to work—if both parents were around and work was to be had. For many of these children, she knew, their school lunch was their main meal of the day.

The chef was smiling at her with his white, even teeth, his clear grey eyes, his freshly shaven skin, and she tightened her fists because he was gorgeous and everything about him expected her to smile back at him.

'Year seven,' she said firmly to the students who were watching them, 'please go back to your seats.'

Reluctantly the students turned back to their chairs and talked among themselves. Angus MacAllister stayed where he was, smiling at her with that smile, looking at her with those eyes. A TV celebrity, waiting for the world to swoon at his feet.

And, of course, Elisabeth wanted to. Because she was a sucker for tall, classy men with cheek and self-confidence and with English accents like that, and she always had been.

But chaos lay in that direction. Unpredictability, risks and danger. Her whole life had been a lesson to resist the urge to follow her impulses.

And the impulse to touch this man was the strongest one she'd ever had in her life.

She folded her arms to make sure she kept her hands to herself.

'I didn't frighten your chicken,' Elisabeth said to Angus MacAllister under cover of the noise. 'And anyway, you shouldn't have an animal like that in a school if it frightens so easily.'

'"Frightens easily" is rather the dictionary definition of the word "chicken",' he said.

Why did his voice hook her, deep in her chest, as if her own body were echoing its gravelly sound?

'And you have to admit that the children are enjoying themselves,' he added. 'Are you?'

She straightened her back. 'I assume this exercise has some sort of educational value?'

'Fun isn't enough, is it, Miss Read? We need an educational aim for everything? Something that can be tested and assessed?'

His words were teasing. Who'd made a chef the expert on education, anyway?

'You have a point,' she said. 'Maybe we should put "Chasing a Chicken" on the national curriculum.'

He laughed, his smile getting broader, and she had to look away before she melted. She glanced down and saw Angus MacAllister's hands again.

And she didn't just want to touch him. She wanted him to touch her.

She wanted one of his hands to grasp her hip, its fingers reaching to the small of her back. She wanted the other one to slide up her waist, under her blouse, the palm stroking her ribs, and then curling round the side of her breast.

Okay. Either her parents' capricious genes had suddenly taken effect in her at twenty-six years of age, or she had lost her mind. She didn't know this man. She'd never even tried one of his recipes. And she was in a classroom full of children.

She needed to get a grip, and fast.

'Did Tasha Cutter arrange for you to speak with her class?' she asked, keeping her voice neutral and professional. 'It's a wonderful opportunity for these students to meet somebody who's made a success of himself.' She smiled at him, tight-lipped and cold. 'Where is their teacher, by the way?'

'I arranged this visit myself. And Tasha just popped out for a moment. I assured her I could keep control until she got back.' His eyes sparkled. 'Of course, I didn't anticipate your turning up and throwing everything into chaos.'

'I didn't—' she started before she realised he was baiting her. 'Well. I'll go find Tasha and let you get on with it, then. Very nice to meet you, Mr MacAllister.'

'Likewise, Miss Read. I'll be sure to look you up if I need any English lessons.' He held out his hand to her.

His half-smile, his eyes steady on hers, let Elisabeth know he was mocking her. Probably because she was acting like a stereo-typed uptight schoolmarm. Possibly because he'd detected her Canadian accent. Maybe—she felt herself flushing all over her body—because he was flirting with her.

And she wanted to touch his hand far too much to let herself touch it.

*It's a handshake, Elisabeth,* she thought. *It's not sex.*

She swallowed, licked her lips, and reached out. Made contact.

His hand was warm, large, wonderful, clever, and, though Elisabeth kept her spine straight, her expression cool, she felt herself going pliant. She wanted to be putty in his hands.

She saw his eyes dip, briefly, to look at her body, and then she knew he was flirting with her.

Oh, he was sure of himself. They were in a room full of children and he still thought he could get anything he wanted. Elisabeth pulled her hand back, nodded at Angus MacAllister, and left the room.

Quickly, before she could forget where she was and who she was, and give him anything he wanted.


A silver convertible screeched to a halt in front of Elisabeth as she stepped outside the school gates.

'I'm taking you for a drive,' Joanna said through the open window. 'We need to talk.' She grabbed a set of exercise books from the front seat and threw them into the back.

Elisabeth climbed in, fastened her seat belt and steeled herself to withstand the constant low-level panic that was endemic to sitting in the passenger seat of Joanna's car.

When Elisabeth had moved to London, she'd discovered most people didn't bother to drive in the capital. It was expensive, and it was dangerous, and it was stressful. Elisabeth's friend Joanna Graham, who since her recent promotion was in charge of Upper School at Slater, seemed to regard it as an extreme sport.

'What do we need to talk about?' Elisabeth asked.

'Among other things, this.' Joanna tossed a leaflet into Elisabeth's lap. She turned the key in the ignition and pulled away from the kerb without discernibly checking her mirrors.

Elisabeth looked down at the leaflet she held in her hand. She read aloud.


'Computer dating. As seen on TV. Having trouble meeting compatable people of the opposite sex? Let our high-tech

computer matching software find your perfect partner!
Success guaranteed. A satisfied customer writes, "I met the
man of my dreams. I'm getting married in two weeks!"'

'See, doesn't it sound great? High-tech and everything.'
Joanna took her eyes off the road to grin at Elisabeth. 'You could
be married within two weeks!'

'They've misspelt 'compatible',' Elisabeth observed.

'So? You hire them for their dating services, not their spell-
checker. Who needs spelling when you can have your soul mate?'

'If my students made that excuse, I'd make them write the
word out fifty times on the board.'

'No you wouldn't. You'd laugh, and then you'd show them a
way to remember how to spell it. That's why you're a good
teacher and I trust you with all my difficult students.' She took
her hands off the wheel to unwrap a chocolate bar.

'You're just trying to flatter me so I'll do what you want.
Where did you get this idea, anyway?'

Joanna held out the chocolate to Elisabeth. 'Want a bite?'
Elisabeth shook her head. 'The leaflet came through the letter-
box with the free papers last night. I took one look and knew it
was for you.'

Elisabeth did not believe in computer-dating services. She
didn't believe in soul mates, come to that. What she told her
students was exactly what she believed herself: your life is controlled by you, by the choices and the mistakes that you make.

It wasn't up to computers, or luck, or karma. Her parents
believed in karma and look what kind of life they had—living in
the middle of the Canadian woods, wearing hemp and eating
lentils and dancing naked in the moonlight, with no conception
of security or the future.

'It's not for me,' Elisabeth said.

Joanna put her hand on Elisabeth's, and looked serious for a
change. 'Elisabeth, you are a dear friend and a great colleague
and a fantastic teacher and it is killing me to see you living the
life of a nun. You need to lighten up. Meet some new people.
Have some fun.'

'I have fun all the time. You should've seen my year nines acting out 'The Charge of the Light Brigade' today. I nearly wet myself, it was so funny.'

'I mean fun outside of school.'

She thought. 'Well, you and I drank all those margaritas last week and watched *Moulin Rouge.* That was fun.'

'I mean fun with a man.'

Fun with a man. Right. Robin had offered her fun, and she'd mistaken it for everything she'd ever wanted. Stupid girl.

'There's more to a relationship than fun,' she said. 'Like decency and commitment and shared goals and values.'

Though sparring with Angus MacAllister over a chicken this morning had been sort of fun. In the spare second or two when she'd been able to avoid thinking about jumping his bones.

She pushed the thought aside.

'Okay, I know Robin was a jerk, and I understand the once-bitten-twice-shy thing,' Joanna said. 'But there are other men in the universe. How many men have you gone out with in the past year?'

'Four.'

'Four,' Jo repeated. 'And were these four hot, sexy men who took you to bed, preferably two at a time, and fulfilled all your wildest fantasies?'

Elisabeth ticked them off on her fingers. 'I went for dinner with Tim the systems analyst; I went for coffee with Mike the corporate lawyer; I saw an opera with Richard the museum curator, and two months ago I went to the Globe with…' She furrowed her brow. 'I can't actually remember what his name was.'

'I bet you remember the play, though.'

'*Romeo and Juliet.* It was wonderful.'

Jo snorted. 'You watched the most romantic play in the world with a man and you can't remember his name. I think your dating choices leave a lot to be desired.'

Elisabeth watched the street signs and shop fronts whiz by. 'They were all very nice men. Steady. Intelligent. Responsible.'

'And you never saw any of them again. I hate to contradict you, Liz, but you're not looking for someone decent and responsible. If you were, you would have seen one of those four men again.'

Joanna shoved the rest of the chocolate bar into her mouth and sped through an intersection just as the light turned red. 'You need to meet someone new. Someone with *zing*.'

'I don't think *"zing"* is a word.'

Even as she said it Elisabeth knew she was prevaricating. Word or not, she knew what *zing* was. She was still feeling the after-effects of the *zing*.

And that was what was scary. Because even with Robin— even with the man she'd completely lost her heart and body to, the one who'd made her forget her judgement and every single thing she valued—she hadn't felt as stunned, as *zinged*, as she had for the few minutes she'd had with Angus MacAllister.

'I'm not going to do any computer dating,' she said firmly.

Joanna shrugged. 'Okay, your loss. How about a personal ad?'

'No.'

'They do speed dating at the pub round the corner from my house.'

'Absolutely not.'

'How about I just set you up with my cousin? He's hot. If we weren't related, I'd be in there myself.'

Elisabeth sighed. 'Jo, is it possible that the outrageous amounts of refined sugar that you consume have made you go completely doolally?'

Jo approached a roundabout and, as usual, braked at the last moment so Elisabeth had to brace herself to avoid being choked by the seat belt.

'I'm not doolally,' Jo said, entering the roundabout directly in the path of a taxi that had to swerve to avoid her. 'I'm just looking out for your future. Somebody has to. Listen, if you don't like my cousin, I know this other guy I used to work with who I think you would like.'

'Stop it,' Elisabeth protested, but now she was laughing. Jo lived the carefree, single, have-a-good-time lifestyle to the maximum: sports car, great clothes, a new man every week, it seemed. Elisabeth admired her for doing it, if it made her happy. She knew it wasn't for her.

She was jolted out of her amusement by Joanna turning a corner so sharply that Elisabeth was thrown against the car door. 'Are you trying to give me whiplash?'

'This car corners like it's on rails, it's great. Listen, Liz, I've got a favour to ask of you.'

'What is it?' Elisabeth asked warily.

'It's a year ten thing.'

At school, Joanna was Head of Upper School, ages fourteen to sixteen, and, despite the fact that she was shorter than most of the boys and some of the girls, most of the three hundred students she was responsible for looked up to her. She was friendly but strict in school; Elisabeth often wondered what her students would make of her if they knew their fearsome teacher was a party girl in her free time. But Jo was scrupulous about keeping her personal life and her professional life separate.

'It might take quite a bit of time,' Jo said, 'but I think it could be really important.'

'What is it?' Elisabeth asked again, but this time with interest. When it came to school, Jo was always right. She was young to hold such an important management role, but she'd earned it because she took an intense interest in all of the students under her care and went to any length to make sure they succeeded.

'I need you to work with Angus MacAllister. You know, the TV chef?'

# CHAPTER TWO

ELISABETH forgot about her grip on the sides of the seat.

'Did you say Angus MacAllister?'

'Yeah. You've heard of him, right? Fantastic chef. I tried his recipe for treble-chocolate espresso cake. Amazing.'

'You want me to *work* with him?'

'Isn't it great? I knew you'd be pleased. It's not every day we get a celebrity in the school, is it?'

'Why me?'

'You mean, besides that I want to give you the glamorous jobs because you're my friend?'

'Yes, besides that.'

Elisabeth could tell Joanna was serious because she slowed the car down.

'You're the only member of staff I think could pull it off. I trust you. You're willing to try anything that might help a student. And if this works, it could make a huge difference to these particular kids.'

Damn Joanna. She was capitalising on Elisabeth's professional pride. 'Which kids?'

'Jennifer Keeling and Danny Williams.'

Ah. She was starting to see what Joanna was getting at.

Elisabeth taught Jennifer, and everybody at the Slater School knew Danny Williams. Jennifer was terminally shy, and Danny was an attention-seeker on his way to leaving school with no qualifications in anything except petty theft and intimidation. Two problem kids on two opposite ends of the behaviour spectrum.

'What about Jennifer and Danny?' Elisabeth said, intrigued now in spite of herself.

'I'm worried about them. Jennifer needs something to make her feel good about herself; I don't think she gets any help at home. Danny needs something to take an interest in, something he can succeed at and see a tangible reward for, and that will steer him towards a job for when he leaves school. And, incredible as it might seem, they're both good at the same thing. Cooking.'

'They're good cooks?' The idea didn't fit the impression she had of either kid.

'Yeah. Tasha told me, and I observed them both in a lesson.'

'Danny Williams. Taking food technology.' She pictured grease fires, egg ambushes. 'You're joking, right?'

'It was the only thing he could take after the business studies department banned him. You remember that internet pornography incident? Anyway, I watched them both and I couldn't believe their focus. They're talented.'

Elisabeth thought about this for a few moments. They were stuck in traffic now, which gave her some calm. 'So what does this have to do with me and Angus MacAllister?'

'It's the most fantastic thing. When I learned about their skills, I got Danny and Jennifer to enter the Kid Culinaire competition. Apparently it's this huge big-deal prestigious competition, and the first prize is admission to Britain's best catering college. Even the runners-up usually get offered a place on a course. Can you imagine what even participating in this contest, let alone winning, would do for Jennifer's self-esteem? And Danny's sense of direction?'

She could imagine it. With luck, it could turn these kids' lives around.

'And Angus MacAllister?' she repeated.

'The school was approached by MacAllister's publicist, who got our details from the competition organiser. MacAllister wants to volunteer his time to help some kids with the competition. I haven't told the kids yet, because it's not definite, but he seems interested in the Slater School. He likes the location and the fact that we're entering two students rather than just one.'

'MacAllister is doing it for the publicity, right?' she said. 'To make himself look good-hearted and child-loving?'

Joanna shrugged. 'Who cares why he's doing it?'

'I care. I'm not eager to let our students be a publicity vehicle for someone who only cares about his own fame.'

Joanna looked sharply at her. 'Whoa. You sound like you've got something against this man already. You don't know him, do you?'

Elisabeth didn't want to admit she'd met Angus this afternoon, because she'd have to admit that she'd felt that incredible attraction to him.

'I'm just concerned about our students, that's all,' she said, making her voice sound nonchalant. 'The last thing Jennifer and Danny need is to be made into a media circus.'

And the last thing Elisabeth needed was to spend any more time with Angus MacAllister.

'So you see one reason why I need you to help with this thing, if it goes through. I need someone to be there when Angus is with the kids, to make sure they're getting the full benefit of this deal.'

'Why not Tasha? I don't know anything about food.'

Joanna snorted. 'Yeah, and that's why you're so skinny, you don't eat anything.' She put the car back into gear and roared away from the traffic light. 'Ostensibly, it's because Tasha's the main care provider for her sick mother, and she's not able to spend that much time after school helping the kids. Between you and me, it's also because she's not so great at keeping discipline. She can barely control Danny as it is, and she's not having much luck talking with Jenny. And if she can't handle a couple of teenagers, how's she going to keep an eye on a fully grown man with his own agenda?'

Joanna shuddered, and smiled. 'Actually that's probably all Tasha would do: keep an eye on the fully grown man. He's pretty fully grown. And very manly. I had a hard time keeping my eyes off him myself.'

'You met him?'

'Oh, yeah. He's very attractive.'

A funny feeling burned in Elisabeth's chest. She ignored it. 'I saw his show once and I didn't think he was that special.'

'He's special, all right. And a charmer. If I didn't know better, I'd think he was interested in me.'

The funny feeling got funnier. It was, incredibly and stupidly, jealousy. Elisabeth tried to swallow it down. Being jealous of a man whom she didn't even like being interested in her friend was just wrong, for more reasons than she could count.

'What do you mean, if you didn't know better?'

Jo laughed. 'Unlike you, I like to take a break from Shakespeare and read gossip magazines. Angus MacAllister is linked with a different woman every week. The man flirts as easily as he makes soufflé.'

Elisabeth remembered Angus's eyes on her, assessing her as if she were a box of fresh, ripe tomatoes. A rush of heat went through her, and that feeling, unlike jealousy, she couldn't suppress.

If she ended up working with Angus MacAllister, what other feelings was he going to arouse in her? Feelings she'd tried so hard, and so successfully, to stay away from for the past few years?

She cleared her throat. 'So you want me to protect Jennifer and Danny from a superficial man who's only interested in what he can get.'

Joanna blinked. 'I didn't say that. I said I wanted you to make sure the kids got everything out of this experience that they could. And that means helping Angus as well as helping Jennifer and Danny. The two of them aren't easy to get on with. And I'm not sure they'll get on with each other, either.'

She pulled the car up in front of Elisabeth's block of flats, scraping the tyres on the kerb. Then she turned to Elisabeth.

'You're the best person for the job, Elisabeth. You have a good reputation with the kids. I sounded out Danny about teachers; he thinks most of us hate him, but he said you were fair to him when you'd dealt with him before.'

Elisabeth remembered a run-in she'd had with Danny on the school playground last year when a window had been broken. The boy had been almost surprised when she'd asked for his side of the story. In that case, he'd been innocent. Not that he usually was. But trouble kids usually expected to get the blame for everything that went wrong; it was one of the reasons they didn't see the point of behaving properly.

'And I know you've made some headway with Jennifer already,' Jo continued. 'She likes you.'

Jennifer had actually smiled in a lesson the week before, when Elisabeth had quietly praised her work. That one small smile had kept Elisabeth happy for days.

'I like her,' Elisabeth said.

'I know it's extra hours,' Jo said. 'And you're not interested in cooking. But you *care*. You could really make the difference between this being a success or not.'

She *cared*.

Elisabeth tightened her fingers on her skirt. Yes, she cared. Her students were just about the only thing she had left to care about.

She could only touch their lives at school. It was limited contact, limited caring. She only had so much influence. Sometimes she could help, and sometimes she had to stand there and watch as they made the wrong choices, fell victim to circumstances of their lives that she couldn't change.

Being a teacher and caring was frustrating and heartbreaking and wonderful, and, for the past two years at least, those were the truest emotions she'd let herself feel. The only ones she *could* feel.

She cared enough about her students to face any demon of hell, let alone a chicken-chasing chef.

'All right,' she said. 'I'll do it.'

Angus leaned back in his wooden chair and prepared to savour the sweet, molten-hot, devil-strong espresso on the table before him.

He took a sip. Ah-h-h-h, paradise. His taste buds sent a welcome shock of coffee-induced pleasure to his brain, and his nerves started tingling back into life.

It had been ten long hours since his last coffee, made for himself on the gleaming espresso machine at his restaurant Magnum at six o'clock this morning. He'd drunk it alone in the empty dining room, going through his notes on some seasonal menu changes he'd wanted to discuss with his *sous chef* Henry before the prep for lunch.

But he hadn't had the chance to talk with Henry, because the minute Henry had arrived he'd told Angus that the order of langoustines they'd based their lunchtime menu on had failed to arrive because there had been an accident on the M25 and traffic had been backed up practically all the way to Dover, and that two of their *commis chefs* were down with the flu, and the upshot of all this was that Angus had spent forty-five minutes on the phone and then ended up driving across London in rush-hour traffic, and then back to Magnum with his vintage Jaguar filled with boxes of ice and shellfish, and had then changed into whites and run the kitchen for a fully booked lunch service.

He'd just hung up his whites, washed his face, and sat down in his office with a bowl of the bouillabaisse from lunch when his phone had rung. He had answered it with a spoonful of soup halfway to his mouth. It had been Christine, his publicist.

'I need to talk to you about the Kid Culinaire school thing,' she said without preamble.

'I'm fine, Christine, how are you?' He eyed the langoustine floating in the saffron-scented soup. If his Jag was going to smell of langoustines for the foreseeable future, it only seemed fair that he should be able to eat one of them while it was hot. But Christine had that tone in her voice that meant she was about to tell him something for his own good. He lowered his spoon.

'Fine. Listen. I've done more negotiations with the three schools you've visited. St Teresa's is eager to work with us, they're fine for TV cameras, but the school is right the other side of London. Gladstone School is also fine with the cameras. But the student has already had private cookery lessons. The Slater School has the kind of kids we're looking for, kids who could use help. But the school is being cagey—they say it's fine to use the school's name and to film the competition, but they don't want the students' names to become public until then, and they want to wait and see how it goes before they have TV cameras in school. And they've made it a condition that you work with a teacher at all times and don't have unsupervised contact with the children.'

'They think I'll be a bad influence on the nation's impressionable youth, eh? Maybe you're to blame for that, Christine, with the stories you've fed to the press about me and all those women.'

Christine was obviously ignoring his teasing today. 'So the Slater School is the best choice for the kids, and it's closest to you, but it's not so great on the publicity front.'

Angus let out an exasperated breath. 'Let's cancel the whole thing. I never wanted to go into a school anyway. My school years were the most miserable of my life—why would I want to spend more time at one?'

'To raise your profile. People love compassionate celebrities.'

He snorted. 'I'm a chef. I do unspeakable things with knives and dead animals on a daily basis. I'm a nice guy, but I don't have time for random compassion. I can barely manage to feed myself.' He stirred his spoon through his cooling soup.

'You do want to be famous, don't you?'

'Um.'

How to explain it? He wanted to be good at what he did, so good that people smiled when they heard his name. He wanted to walk into rooms and have people want to know him. To have their faces light up because he was there, because he was important to them, because he mattered.

None of that was being famous, precisely. But fame was the closest to it that he'd found. Fame, and work, made some progress into filling what was empty in him, what had been empty for as long as he remembered.

'Do you really think this is a good idea?' he asked, bypassing the difficult question.

'Yes. The market is inundated with chefs. You're the best-looking of the lot, but you need something else to make you stand out. Helping children and working for charity are hot right now.'

And cooking skills didn't seem to come into it.

Oh, well. It wasn't as if he didn't use his appearance and his skills for promotional purposes anyway. More publicity would allow him to develop his restaurant, to further his career.

Why did it have to be in a school, though? The one place that was guaranteed to push his buttons?

He sighed. *Stop it, MacAllister. You're not that pathetic kid any more.*

'All right,' he said, going back to business mode. 'It looks like we can eliminate the Slater School if they're so shy about publicity and they're imposing rules. Who's the teacher they want me to work with, anyway?'

'Her name's Elisabeth Read. She doesn't even teach cooking; she teaches English.'

Angus dropped his spoon and sat up straight in his chair.

Elisabeth Read. The English teacher with the North American accent, the person who'd sent MacNugget into a panic yesterday and then sized Angus up and ordered him around.

The bossy Miss Read. The prim Miss Read. The beautiful Miss Read, with her straight posture thrusting her breasts forward against her clinging top. Her glossy brown hair had been swept up at her nape, revealing an elegant neck. And best of all: her delicate chin was set, her brown eyes sparked, and her coral lips pushed forward in the semblance of a kiss.

The annoyed, and very sexy, Miss Read.

'I'll work with the Slater School,' he said.

'But the publicity opportunities aren't—'

'They're good enough,' he interrupted. 'Set me up a meeting with Miss Read this afternoon at Luciano's.'

So here he was at Luciano's Italian Coffee Bar three hours later, after lukewarm bouillabaisse and then mediocre tea at a meeting with his investors, waiting for Miss Read.

Angus took another blissful sip of espresso and conjured up her perfume. Orange and cinnamon, exotic and warm. Her hair smelled of caramel. If he could capture the smell in flavours, he'd never stop eating. As it was, he wanted to sink more than his teeth into her.

Another thing he liked in a woman: competence and control. She hadn't been rattled by his panicked chicken, or the students running around with wooden spoons. She'd responded to his teasing with polished-crystal dignity.

The only thing that had rattled her was his touch. She'd blushed as soon as he'd held out his hand, the only sign that she'd been feeling the same attraction that he had.

He knocked back the remainder of his espresso and signalled the waiter for another.

With caffeine and sugar in his bloodstream, he could think more clearly. What was he doing, agreeing to this publicity stunt he didn't have time for, doing something he had no interest in?

He was no teacher. He did some training with chefs in his kitchen, but they were professionals who barked, 'Yes, Chef!' to his every order. His TV shows broke down recipes and showed viewers what to do, which was like teaching, he supposed, but TV viewers didn't talk back and mess around. He knew from his time in the classroom yesterday that if you turned your back on kids for a second, they had the weapons out and were trapping some poor cowering animal in a corner.

Not so different from his own schooldays, actually. He could remember being that cowering animal. Alone, scared, vulnerable, with not even a safe cage to return to.

He shook his head. What was he getting himself into? Five seconds into this project and he was remembering things he'd thought he'd put behind him long ago. All because he had the hots for a woman.

He didn't have time for women, either. Yes, he knew a lot of them, a lot of beautiful, intelligent, witty ones, and he went with them to restaurants and openings and parties, because you had to do these things and it was much more enjoyable with an interesting and aesthetically pleasing person beside you.

The tabloids implied that he was sleeping with all of them, and that usually made Angus laugh. Sometimes he felt like turning up at their offices and handing the tabloid editors a copy of his schedule: the eighteen-hour days he put in at Magnum and the studio, the hours he spent at home writing and planning, the nights he worked through to morning and shaved and put on fresh clothes and went back to his restaurant.

When was he supposed to fit in sex? He had time for a five-minute fumble in a closet, maybe.

For Angus, sex was more than a five-minute fumble. Sex was like food, fine wine, something to be enjoyed slowly, with every sense, worth all the effort and time. For sex you needed the right ingredients. The right setting, the right woman. And all the skill and attention you could lavish on it.

English teacher Miss Elisabeth Read was, for whatever reason, the right ingredient.

Angus leaned further back into the chair, stretching his legs out beneath the table and clasping his hands behind his neck. Who would've thought he would ever have the hots for a teacher? He laughed quietly and pictured it.

*Miss Read leaned forward over her desk, breasts straining against a prissy blouse, undone to show her glorious cleavage. She frowned, and then ran her tongue over moist, glossy lips.*

*'You've been naughty, MacAllister,' she growled, lowering her eyelids seductively. 'I need to see you after the lesson.* Do you need another coffee to wake you up?'

Angus, smiling broadly with his eyes closed, realised that the voice in his head had become real.

He opened his eyes to see Miss Strict Schoolteacher transformed into the actual Miss Elisabeth Read, looking considerably less welcoming than she had in his fantasy. She wore a chocolate-brown top, loose crème-caramel linen trousers, and dangly turquoise earrings. Her hair fell straight down over her shoulders. Her eyes, the same colour as her jumper, regarded him with wariness.

He stood and held out his hand. 'Elisabeth, I'm glad to see you again.'

For the second before she shook his hand he anticipated the pleasure of touching her, and then his hand was wrapped around hers again. Her skin was smooth, soft, her grip strong. She wore a chunky silver moonstone ring. The tips of her fingers were cold, but her palm was warm. He wondered if she was like her hand: cold on the outside, warm and welcoming and passionate on the inside.

'Mr MacAllister. Thank you for meeting me.' She withdrew her hand, and though he searched for the awareness he'd seen in her eyes the last time they'd touched, she was hiding it better now.

'Call me Angus.' He reached round the tiny table and pulled her chair out for her. 'What would you like to drink?'

'Oh.' Her smooth forehead creased slightly as she thought

about it. 'Just a filter coffee, please, with skim milk if they've got it.' She sat down.

If she had to think about an order like that, it was because it wasn't what she really wanted.

'Luciano,' Angus called to the old man behind the bar, '*un cappuccino, per favore.* So,' he said, sitting down across from Elisabeth, 'I didn't bring MacNugget with me today. What do you think we should talk about?'

Her forehead creased more. 'Thank you, but I didn't want a cappuccino.'

'Coming to Luciano's and ordering filter coffee is like going to the Louvre and asking for a comic book,' Angus said. 'A comic book is fine, but you're missing the Mona Lisa. Trust me. You want a cappuccino.'

She stocd. 'I'll just change my order. Excuse me.'

As she passed him Angus stood and touched her arm. This time, he heard her sharp intake of breath and knew that she was as affected as he was by the contact.

'Elisabeth,' he said, keeping his voice low, feeling how close she was, 'Luciano makes espresso that tastes like velvet and feels like a freight train. For a cappuccino, he adds hot frothy milk and tops it with chocolate that tastes like a sweet, gentle kiss.'

She was frozen to the spot, her eyes as dark and rich as the espresso he'd been talking of. Their pupils were wide.

She smelled of caramel and oranges. Her lips would taste better than any cappuccino. It was only the two of them in the crowded café. Her body was graceful and still, mere inches from his, her face tilted up towards him.

Angus couldn't remember the last time he'd felt like this. Just the feeling of her arm, the scent and warmth of her and the word 'kiss' in his mouth, and his blood was pounding, his groin tightening. It wasn't difficult to turn Angus on. But so quickly, with barely a touch…

Absolutely brilliant.

'Come on, Elisabeth,' he murmured. 'Trust me.'

And just like that the spell was broken. She blinked and pulled her arm out of his grasp. 'Excuse me,' she said again, her voice a tiny bit breathy, so slight he would have missed it if he hadn't been listening for it.

Angus watched her walk to the counter. Her posture was straight, her hips swaying slightly as she moved.

The woman was stubborn and she had wonderful self-control. Her will was probably as iron-strong as his.

He liked her a lot.

Of course, she didn't seem to like him.

But Angus wasn't worried about that. He was good at making people like him. It was a skill you picked up fast when you were abandoned at boarding-school at six years old.

He'd perfected the skill in every wretched expensive boarding-school he'd been sent to for the next ten years, every busy exciting kitchen he'd worked in after that. Work hard at what you're good at, and make people like you. It was the only way to survive.

She came back with a filter coffee and a cappuccino, which she set down in front of him. 'Since you ordered it I thought you'd probably like it,' she said, sitting again.

Angus threw back his head and laughed. 'Well done, Miss Read. I like it when a woman can put me in my place.' He raised the frothy cappuccino in a toast to her. 'Here's to skim milk.'

At that, she cracked a smile. Not much of one, but to Angus it was a prize, the first and smallest of victories.

'You're Canadian?' he said, thinking it was about time he risked a personal question.

'My parents are naturalised Canadians. I was brought up in Canada. I'm British now.' It was said with a firmness that declared the subject closed. 'And please don't make the comment about a person from Canada teaching English.'

'I wouldn't dream of it.' Elisabeth Read's defences were well rehearsed. He wondered why she'd chosen to work with him.

He took a sip of his cappuccino. It was as good as he'd said it was. As he licked off the foam that clung to his lip he saw her eyes dip to his mouth. Then her own lovely mouth compressed and she looked back at her own coffee. She was attracted to him, and she was determined not to be. He had a feeling she wanted the cappuccino, too. Intriguing.

'So we're going to be working together,' he said. 'Are you interested in cooking?'

'No, I'm interested in children. Joanna Graham asked me to help with this competition because we want Jennifer and Danny to benefit from it just as much as you do.'

He smiled and settled back in his chair. 'I see. You don't trust me with the children.'

'I'm sure you're a consummate professional, Mr MacAllister. But these children have particular needs that must be addressed, and I'm not sure that your publicity campaign will take those into account.'

*What about your needs, Elisabeth?* 'Please call me Angus.'

'Angus, then. May I speak confidentially, with the understanding that this won't be picked up by your publicist or the press?'

'Of course.'

She rested her elbows on the table and leaned forward towards him. Her arms were long and slender, and he could see the delicate knobs of her wrists. He loved that part of a woman, so fragile and flexible, near where the pulse beat, as erotic as the soft hollow underneath her ears, or the curve of her belly.

He had the feeling Elisabeth had erotic places he'd never even imagined before.

'Jennifer and Danny are both vulnerable children who are having trouble in school. We want them to participate in this contest to build their self-esteem and to give them some hope that they can succeed in something after they've finished their exams next year. But they're both going to be difficult to help, for different reasons. Jennifer is withdrawn, and Danny reacts to authority with aggression. When they're confronted with anything difficult, Jennifer is likely to give up trying right away and Danny usually resorts to destructive attention-seeking.'

And just like that, talking about her students, Elisabeth Read had transformed from the controlled, cold woman she'd been a moment ago. Her movements were looser, earnest, her hands punctuating her points. She met his eye, and kept it.

She really did care about these kids, passionately.

'All the tests show that Jennifer is an intelligent girl,' she continued, 'but she's so afraid of social contact that she finds it impossible to succeed at schoolwork. I've taught her for two years and have hardly heard more than two sentences out of her. She doesn't appear to have any friends.

'Danny, on the other hand, has a lot of friends, and all of them are troublemakers. He has some learning difficulties and this made him the target of bullies when he first came to the school. So he joined them. He's failing all of his subjects.' She took a sip of her coffee. 'They're both going to need careful handling if we're going to succeed with them. But Joanna Graham and I both believe that this contest could make a big difference in their lives.'

Angus forgot about his coffee. He understood now why he had the hots for this teacher. It wasn't only her beauty, her will, her straight-backed grace. It was this passion bubbling under her controlled surface. Passion that, right now, was directed at her students' welfare.

He knew a lot of people who were passionate about food, or about fame. It had been a long time since he had met somebody who was passionate about people. He wasn't sure if he ever had.

And having learned this about Elisabeth, he could imagine her passion directed at other things. Him, for example.

Angus MacAllister was staring at her.

He'd been looking at her before; he'd been flirting with her. But now he was downright staring.

All of the ease she'd rediscovered while she was talking about her pupils left her, and Elisabeth felt like she had fifteen minutes ago, when he'd touched her. Powerless in the face of her yearning. Barely able to breathe.

She fought to regain the thread of what she'd been saying. She'd been talking about the kids. Why would he stare at her like that when she was talking about students he didn't even know? It wasn't as if what she was saying could matter to him.

'Excuse me, but aren't you Angus MacAllister?'

The interruption broke the spell she was under, and Elisabeth looked up to see a middle-aged woman standing next to their table. She was smiling nervously at Angus.

'Yes, hello,' Angus said, rising and offering his hand to the woman.

'I'm such a big fan of yours,' said the woman, blushing as she shook his hand. 'I had to come over and say hello.'

'Thank you.' He was beaming at her, and Elisabeth noticed that he appeared to be one-hundred-per-cent sincere, despite the fact that a second ago he'd been giving Elisabeth all of his attention. 'That's kind of you. I appreciate it. What's your name?'

'Helen.' The woman was clearly delighted at his attention.

'I'm very pleased to meet you, Helen. Are you enjoying Luciano's coffee as much as I am?'

Elisabeth watched him charm the woman, chat with her, ask her questions about herself, accept her compliments with cheerful grace. So this was what it was like to be famous. You had to suffer interruptions, invasions of privacy, and appear to love it.

Then again, he probably did love it, she thought as Angus asked Luciano for a pen to sign the paper napkin the woman asked him to autograph. Personally, she couldn't imagine anything worse. Growing up surrounded by people, in shared houses and hippy communes across the breadth of Canada, she'd learned to guard her privacy, hoard every inch of personal space, treasure the times she could choose whom to share her thoughts with.

She understood the need to have a public persona—that was what you did in the classroom, after all. But if you had to be in public all the time, how on earth could you tell who you really were? How could you feel secure over your own life if you let other people have access to it whenever they wanted?

Maybe you became your public persona, your famous self. She wouldn't have been surprised if that was what Robin was like all the time these days, for example.

Angus shook the woman's hand again, and she went back to her table as he took his seat. 'Sorry about that.' He grinned at Elisabeth. 'Hazard of the profession.'

And he'd dealt with it as if it were as easy and natural as breathing.

'This is one of the things I wanted to talk with you about,' she said. 'Jennifer and Danny are vulnerable enough without being made the focus of national press attention. We will not allow their names or images to be used for publicity without the permission of their parents and the school. This permission may never be granted. If you talk about what you're doing with the press, you'll have to respect their need for anonymity.'

Angus frowned.

'Of course.' For the first time since she'd met him, his voice betrayed some other emotion than cheerful self-confidence. He almost sounded angry. She supposed it must be a shock for him to hear her laying down the law, after Helen's adoration.

'I've agreed to the school's conditions, and I'll respect them,' he said.

'Good.' Elisabeth finished her coffee and stood, putting her cup back on its saucer. 'I know you're a busy man, Mr MacAllister, so I'll let you get back to your work. I'm glad we had this chance to talk and that we understand each other.'

Though as she said it, she knew she was being as insincere as he must have been when he'd talked with his fan. She and Angus MacAllister came from two different worlds. They didn't understand each other, and they never would.

# CHAPTER THREE

HER palms were sweating, her knees felt shaky, and her stomach was doing rapid rollovers.

It was silly. Elisabeth didn't know why she was feeling so nervous. She'd made it through most of the pivotal moments of her life without getting all knock-kneed: her valedictorian speech at high school, her interview for her scholarship to Cambridge, moving to England by herself at age eighteen, standing in front of a classroom for the first time. She was usually level-headed and clear-thinking and her stomach did not usually try to climb out of her throat.

As she walked from her classroom towards Reception, where she was going to meet Angus and sign him into school for his first lesson with Jennifer and Danny, a tiny traitorous voice spoke in her head.

*You have felt this way before, you know. This is exactly the way you felt before your first date with Robin, nearly three years ago.*

Elisabeth pushed the voice aside and wiped her hands on her skirt, which was slim-fitting and which she *hadn't* chosen because she was going to see Angus today.

Just as she hadn't been thinking about seeing him again ever since their meeting in the café yesterday. Just as late last night she hadn't lain in bed alone and thought about what she would do if Angus walked in, miraculously, like an answer to a dream, and climbed in with her. His long, hard body beside hers; his voice, low and throaty, as it had been in the café when he'd told her to trust him about the coffee. And his hands.

Yeah. She hadn't thought about it at all.

Had she been this obsessive about Robin? Since the awful ending to their affair, she'd done her best not to think about it. But the scary truth was that, actually, she suspected she probably hadn't even thought about Robin this much.

She rounded the corner to the reception area and there he was, chatting with the receptionist. Harjeet was clearly starstruck; she gazed up at Angus adoringly as he said something.

Nothing new for Angus MacAllister. The way he acted, he expected every woman to worship him. She wiped her hands on her skirt one more time and stepped forward.

'Elisabeth.' She was no sooner in the room than Angus stood in front of her, his hand around hers, his grey eyes and his scent and his warmth and tallness overwhelming her again.

'Nice to see you, Angus,' she said, although it wasn't nice to see him. It was wonderful and terrible.

'It's brilliant to see you, Elisabeth.' Her name on his tongue was like a caress. 'Where are the kids? I'm eager to meet them.'

Uh-huh. And she was the Faerie Queene. He was eager to start his publicity push, more like it.

'They'll be in the food technology room in a few minutes,' she said, keeping her tone friendly while she went through the sign-in formalities and got him a visitor's badge. Harjeet, she noticed, never once took her eyes off the chef.

Angus clipped his badge onto the collar of his jacket. He was wearing more casual clothes than the last two times she'd seen him: worn but spotless jeans, a loose T-shirt with the England football logo on it, trainers, and a battered brown leather jacket. He carried a black backpack.

'Nice to meet you, Harjeet, and good luck with the renovations,' he called, and followed Elisabeth down the hallway.

'Renovations?'

'Harjeet's husband is redoing their bathroom. She's a little frightened about his lack of plumbing skills.'

'Oh. I'm sorry. I must've kept you waiting for a long time.'

'No, I'd only just arrived.'

He'd only just arrived and he knew all about Harjeet's

husband's plumbing? She glanced at him to see if he was having her on, but he didn't look any more mischievous than usual. 'How'd you find that out?'

He shrugged. 'Just chatting. So how's your day been?'

*Filled with thoughts of you.* 'Fine, thanks. Have you given any thought to what I said about Jennifer and Danny?'

'It's all I've been thinking about,' he said cheerfully. 'I'm very excited about the challenge. I don't get many opportunities like this, you know.'

She glanced at his face. He'd charmed Harjeet within seconds, and now, she was sure, he was trying to charm her by acting enthusiastic about this project when he was anything but. But his expression was open, and his tone held no trace of sarcasm.

'Neither do the kids,' she said cautiously, and opened the door to the food technology room. Good. They were here before the students, which gave them a better chance of establishing a safe territory for Jennifer and well-defined rules for Danny.

Children and adolescents appreciated definite boundaries and rules. She knew this particularly, since she'd grown up with so few of them herself.

And it gave Elisabeth a few more minutes to attempt to calm down her raging hormones. 'So,' she said, 'keeping in mind what we talked about yesterday, I think it could be a good idea to—'

'Why are you angry at me, Elisabeth?'

She'd been heading for the centre of the classroom, putting some distance between herself and Angus, taking control of the room. But at his words she stopped.

'Um.'

She'd expected him to say all the charismatic, insincere, famous-person things. Not that sudden question.

'I'm not angry,' she said at last. But as soon as she spoke she knew it wasn't the truth. She was angry as hell. Who did he think he was, coming into her world and doing anything he wanted? When she couldn't? When she had to put up boundaries, control her feelings, do whatever she could so she wouldn't lose herself?

Angus put down his rucksack on a counter and leaned back against it, his tall body comfortable-looking, his grey eyes sharp.

'Yes, you are. You look like you want to punch me in the face. What have I done to upset you? Because I want to stop doing it.'

She swallowed back her anger. He was right; he hadn't done anything. And it wasn't his fault that she couldn't do what she wanted. That was just the way life was. She had inappropriate desires. Hardly surprising, given her background. She just had to deal with them.

'It's not what you've done,' she said. 'It's who you are.'

'What is it about who I am that makes you angry? We've just met, Elisabeth. Do you not like chefs? Or people who keep chickens?' He stepped forward, and spread out his hands in front of him in a helpless gesture. 'I think you should let me know before we start working together. Maybe I can change your mind.'

Oh, God, this was such a stupid idea. She'd hoped she could ignore the way her body felt about Angus, that she could be cold and distant and he would let her be just a teacher in the room. But he was standing like that, his eyes and face open and friendly and appealing, and he wanted her to *like* him, of all things.

'It's not important,' she said, and turned away from him as if she were inspecting the room.

Even without looking at him she knew he'd come closer, because every inch of exposed skin started tingling.

'It is important,' he said, and her skin tingled even more at his husky voice. He was right behind her. Close enough to touch. 'Because—'

There was a tentative knock. Elisabeth, relieved and disappointed in equal measure, saw Jennifer's outline through the frosted glass of the door. 'I'll get that,' she said, and started towards it, but Angus beat her to it with a couple of long-legged strides.

The teenager stood in the doorway, thin and lank-haired, with her eyes cast down.

'You must be Jennifer,' Angus said. He spoke gently. 'I've heard a lot about you, Jennifer, and I'm very pleased to meet you. I'm Angus.'

He extended his hand to her, but when Jennifer shrank back he dropped it and stood aside so she could enter the room without coming close to him. Her gaze flickered to Elisabeth, but then it was back on her shoes as she put her books on a bench and stood there, one of her hands gripping the thumb of the other.

A scared little girl. Elisabeth's heart went out to her. She knew exactly how Jennifer felt.

Talking more with Jo, she'd learned the girl only had one parent, and that one was rarely home. She was practically raising herself. A situation that Elisabeth could definitely relate to.

'Hey, Jennifer,' she said softly, coming to stand beside her, 'I'm so proud you were chosen for this contest. It'll be great to learn from a real chef, won't it?'

Jennifer made a movement of her head that could have been a nod.

Danny arrived wafting stale cigarette smoke that Elisabeth could smell even from a distance. He stood in the doorway, hands shoved deep into the pockets of his trousers, the tie of his school uniform hanging loose around his neck.

'How long is this going to take, anyway?' he said. 'I got stuff to do.'

His voice was surprisingly young-sounding for his slouchy teenage body. He registered Elisabeth's presence and then settled his eyes on Angus. The expression on his face could have been taken for either hostility or fear.

'All right, Dan, glad you're here,' Angus said.

There was something subtly different about Angus; it took a moment for Elisabeth to realise that his accent had relaxed into a slight Scottish sound. Less intimidating than his normal diction.

She saw Danny register Angus's jeans and trainers and his football T-shirt. *Not teacher.* For the first time, Elisabeth wondered if Angus had chosen these clothes specifically to put the kids more at ease.

'Great, we can get started,' Angus said, and rubbed his hands together enthusiastically. With a swift movement he grabbed his bag, took out a bundle of dark cloth, and took it to a table in the centre of the room. 'Come on, I won't hurt you.'

Elisabeth could have sworn Angus directed that comment at her. *Yeah, right,* she thought, and then noticed that both Jennifer and Danny were watching her, waiting for her to take the lead.

Not surprising; she was the familiar element in this whole scenario, and even the little trust they had in her was more than they had in Angus. Although she'd intended to do no such thing, she went to stand near Angus's table, and the students followed.

Angus waited until they were all standing in front of him, quiet and waiting. 'My name's Angus MacAllister,' he said, 'and I like to be called Angus instead of Mr MacAllister or sir. But when you're in this room, you call me one thing. And that is "Chef". Do you understand?'

Jennifer did her tiny nod. Danny shrugged.

Angus looked at Elisabeth. She remembered what he'd said before the kids arrived, about trying to make her change her mind about liking him.

Part of her wanted to keep her mouth shut, defy him to make her respond to him. But she was here for the good of the children, and if this was going to work, they needed her to play along.

So she said what she'd really wanted to say, all along, since she'd first met Angus.

'Yes.'

'Yes, what?'

She smiled a little at that. 'Yes, Chef.'

'Good.' He flashed her one of his smiles before he turned back to the kids. 'Have you watched my television shows?'

Another nod and shrug.

'What's that?' Angus prompted.

'Yes, Chef,' Jennifer and Danny said in self-conscious mumbles.

'Excellent. Did you like them?'

'Yes, Chef.' The second time was easier for them. It would get easier every time, Elisabeth knew. Angus wasn't a teacher, but he knew the teacher trick of subtle, good-natured bullying.

'Brilliant. Thank you.' He checked their faces to make sure he had their full attention, and then his face grew serious.

'I want you to understand something right away,' he said. 'Being a chef is *not* like that TV show. It isn't chucking a lot of things in a pan and then a jump-cut to a finished dish; it isn't a lot of laughing and playing around with the camera. Being a chef is hard work.'

Angus leaned his hands on the table, his face level with the teenagers', his voice quiet and authoritative. 'I've been cooking since I was younger than you two. It has taken me years to get where I am today. I've worked eighteen-hour shifts in kitchens that were like war zones. I've sweated and bled and borrowed a hell of a lot of money to make a name for myself. And the work hasn't ended just because I've got the name.'

He watched them, to make sure what he'd said had sunk in. Jennifer and Danny both looked slightly taken aback, but they were absorbed.

'Do you two want to be chefs?'

As he asked the question Angus looked straight at Danny who, caught unexpectedly, stammered, 'Y-yeah. Chef.'

'Yes, Chef,' Jennifer murmured when Angus directed his gaze at her.

'This is a fresh start,' said Angus. 'Whatever might have happened to you before today, whatever problems you might be having at school or in your life, in here they are gone. I'm not going to judge you for anything that's happened in your past. I don't care about that.'

He'd been speaking to the kids, but with those words Angus looked directly at Elisabeth. And she knew what Jennifer and Danny had felt like when he'd put them on the spot: pinned by the full force of his attention, all of his intensity, helpless to do anything but respond as he wanted.

Except in Elisabeth's case, the feeling was compounded by a rush of sexual desire. And the realisation that he was referring to their earlier conversation, when he'd asked her why she was angry at him when he hadn't done anything.

She swallowed, not trusting herself to say anything in front of the students. Angus looked away.

'For me, all that matters is how well you cook,' he said. 'That's it. I'm going to judge you on your dedication to making good food. Look at these.'

He held his hands out before him, palms up, fingers spread.

For a moment, Elisabeth couldn't tell what he meant. His hands were beautiful. Strong and capable, with long fingers and slightly turned-out thumbs. The most extraordinary hands she'd ever seen, the only hands that had ever made her body respond before she'd ever felt their touch.

But why did he want the kids to look at them?

Then she saw it, what she hadn't been able to see before because she hadn't been looking closely, and she drew in a sharp breath.

His hands were covered in scars from fingertip to wrist.

Some were white and fully healed, some pink and shiny. Some thin, some round. He turned his hands over slowly so they could see that the backs of his hands, and his forearms, were similarly marked.

'If you become a chef, you're going to have hands just like this,' Angus said. 'Knives will cut you; pans will burn you. I won't even go into what a bacon slicer can do. This one—' he ran his right thumb up a jagged scar the entire length of his left index finger '—was caused by a prawn. And if you become a chef, you'll be proud of every scar, because every single one of them taught you something that's made you better.'

Elisabeth couldn't take her eyes off them. She imagined the pain each scar had cost.

She knew about scars. Although none of hers was visible.

'I've been burned plenty of times,' Danny boasted. He held out his own hand to Angus and Elisabeth saw a dark red line across his knuckles. 'Got it off the grill pan.'

'And what did you learn from that?' Angus asked.

'Don't make bacon sandwiches when you're drunk.'

The smile on Danny's face was smug, challenging. *Go ahead, tell me off for under-age drinking,* it said.

'Good lesson,' Angus said blandly instead, and he pushed forward the bundle of cloth he'd put on the table and started unwrapping it.

'I learned early that if I wanted to avoid being hurt, I needed to look after these.' He finished unrolling the cloth and Elisabeth saw that it was a holder for a set of gleaming, silver-coloured knives. 'Jennifer, could you get me an onion and a chopping board, please?'

The shy girl obeyed, placing the items in front of Angus. He smiled thanks, pulled a knife from the collection, and, with a quick movement that Elisabeth barely registered, sliced the onion in half. He continued talking while he peeled the onion and sliced it into paper-thin half-moon shapes.

'A sharp knife cuts things by itself. It requires very little pressure, so it's less likely to slip. A sharp knife will prevent many more accidents than it causes.'

Angus's hands moved like a magician's, taking a whole onion and transforming it into slices seemingly without any effort whatsoever.

'You're not crying,' Elisabeth said, drawn into the spell of watching him.

'That's for two reasons. One, is that this is a very sharp knife. Two, is that I'm not a crier.'

*Well, that's one thing he and I have in common,* Elisabeth thought. She wasn't a crier, either, any more.

He finished slicing the onion and gave the knife to Danny, presenting him with the handle; he pulled out another knife for Jennifer, who held it as if it were alive.

'Miss Read, you look like you need a big one,' he said quietly, his grey eyes sparkling. He pulled out a huge knife and offered it to her.

Elisabeth looked at the knife. It looked like the one in that shower scene in *Psycho*. 'I don't need to learn,' she protested.

'I'm surprised.' His voice was a low, intimate, throaty sound that made the hairs on the back of Elisabeth's neck stand up. 'I thought a good teacher would never pass up an opportunity to learn something new.'

After that, she had no choice. The man was a master manipulator of people as well as cookware. Elisabeth took the knife.

Angus produced a bag of vegetables from one of the fridges and before she knew it Elisabeth found herself julienning a carrot and admiring his teaching style.

She put the enormous knife down to watch him instructing Danny and Jennifer. Their concentration was complete as he praised them and gave them tips. He was gentle with Jennifer, and casual and jokey with Danny. They were learning.

And so was she.

People didn't just like Angus MacAllister because he was a famous, good-looking chef. They liked him because he was a consummate charmer. He went out of his way to pay attention to others. He figured out what would appeal to them. And he had a gift of appearing totally, transparently sincere, as if he actually cared about what he was doing and whom he was talking to.

It must've been a useful skill for him to have in those hours he was sweating and working his way to the top. It was probably useful to him with all those women he was supposed to be seeing, too.

At least she could relax about one thing. Angus MacAllister wasn't flirting with her because he was interested in her. He was doing it because he acted that way with everybody. It was second nature to him.

She picked up the knife and started on another carrot. She could stop worrying about the kids, for now; whatever Angus's motivations were for the future of this project, today he was teaching them.

She let her body settle into her chopping rhythm. Up and down, stack the carrot slices, slice into matchsticks and push into a neat pile. Usually she didn't bother about what her food looked like or how it was cut, but this had a certain satisfaction.

'It'll be easier if you let the knife do the work instead of your arm.' Angus's voice was soft in her ear. She started, nearly dropping the knife.

'You shouldn't sneak up on people who are holding knives.' She glanced back over her shoulder at him; he was only inches away. The knife handle became slick in her suddenly perspiring hands.

'Just trying to help. Here, let me show you.' He stood closer to her and put his arms around her from behind, his hands over her own. His breath tickled her ear and sent a shiver down her spine. 'Just lift your wrist. Let the knife point stay on the board. Like this.'

He guided her hands, his grip firm, gentle, and utterly compelling. Up and down on the board, rocking the knife.

His arms embraced her. His body behind her was hot, tall, controlled strength. She could smell him: lemony aftershave, the onion on his hands, and the sensual smell of himself.

'We didn't get to finish our conversation earlier,' he murmured to her. 'How about we go for another coffee after this? The skim milk's on me.'

She couldn't see his face; she could only see his corded wrists, his ravaged, competent hands. They covered hers completely and controlled her movements.

She checked on the children; Danny was searching through a refrigerator, and Jennifer was working on an apple, watching it closely as she produced a long unbroken spiral of red peel. Thank God.

'No, thank you,' she said.

'See, this is exactly what we need to talk about. You keep on acting the dignified schoolteacher with me. I know there's more to you underneath.'

'And what makes you think that?' she asked, keeping her voice steady.

His breath feathered on her neck before he answered, and sent a thrill down her spine that tightened her breasts, made her nipples harden underneath her thin shirt.

'Because of the way you make me feel,' he said.

Oh-h-h, damn him again.

She knew it was a line. She knew he flattered and flirted. She knew it meant precisely nothing.

But her heart leapt, her breath caught, and her insides melted, because he sounded as if he were telling the truth.

'Stop it,' she said. 'You don't know anything about me.'

'And I want to change that. Come for coffee, dinner, whatever you like. I want to get to know you.'

She watched his hands and hers on the knife. They made a rhythm together. Up, down, up, down, sensual and hypnotic. Slicing the carrot to ribbons.

'Mr MacAllister, there are children in the room, and I don't think this is appropriate.' She twisted her shoulders as if she wanted to shake him off.

He took his hands off hers and stepped back. The desired effect, and yet Elisabeth wanted his arms around her again.

'I agree,' he said quietly. 'So let's go somewhere else together, after we've finished here. If you say no, I'm going to keep on asking until you say yes, so you might as well save us both some time.'

Elisabeth looked around the room again to check if Danny and Jennifer were watching. They were both absorbed in their knife-work. Even if they'd seen, they probably wouldn't think anything of it; Angus's actions would appear like a bit of harmless flirtation to an outside observer. They wouldn't be able to see the full sexual meltdown she'd been going through.

Angus could, though. She could see it when she looked at him; his smile, the invitation in his eyes. Her cheeks felt flushed, her joints loose, and when she glanced down she saw that her hard nipples were visible through her bra and thin top.

Why hadn't she put on a sweater this morning? Or full-body chain mail?

'Don't you want to?' Angus asked.

She crossed her arms over her chest. 'Wanting has nothing to do with it. I'm not going to. Thank you for inviting me.'

His smile was slow and self-assured. 'Wanting has everything to do with it, Elisabeth.'

Cocky so-and-so. Elisabeth reached for another carrot. She lay it down carefully on the chopping board. Then she caught his gaze and held it.

'No, Chef,' she said. And brought her huge knife down onto the carrot, hard, thwacking it in half.

Angus winced.

'I get it,' he said. '"*There is no following her in this fierce vein.*"'

Shakespeare. He was quoting *A Midsummer Night's Dream*. Elisabeth blinked.

'You'll say yes eventually,' Angus said, and grinned at her, and went back to helping the kids.

# CHAPTER FOUR

'ESSENTIALLY *A Midsummer Night's Dream* is about problems with love.'

Elisabeth sat on top of her desk and surveyed her year seven class, most of whom were encountering untranslated Shakespeare for the first time in their lives.

'The characters are in this magical forest where anything can happen. Helena was in love with Demetrius and he didn't love her back. So now, when suddenly he's acting as if he's in love with her, because he's had a spell cast on him by the fairies, she doesn't trust him. She thinks he's making fun of her.'

Jimmy Peto raised his hand and, as usual, started speaking at the same time without waiting for Elisabeth to call on him. 'If Candy Coleman suddenly fell in love with me I wouldn't care, miss. I'd just get with her.'

The class erupted into sniggers. Elisabeth smiled, and quieted the twelve-year-olds with a movement of her hand.

'Well, that's understandable, Jimmy, but think about what happens in the rest of the play, what happens when somebody falls in love with the wrong person. They either make fools of themselves, or they get hurt.'

'Yeah,' said Jimmy. He furrowed his little forehead. 'Love pretty much stinks. It's better to stick with football.'

This time, Elisabeth didn't even try to silence the class. She let them chatter and laugh while they gave in their copies of *A Midsummer Night's Dream* and packed away their things. Best to let the class end on a positive note, and she could do with the two minutes of time before the bell rang for the end of the day. Today was Friday, the day of Angus's sixth lesson with Jennifer and Danny.

Lessons two through five had gone pretty much like lesson one. Angus had turned up, flirted, helped Jennifer and Danny with their cooking, and made Elisabeth cook too. She'd learned how to make Béarnaise, hollandaise, and mayonnaise. She could bake a cake; she could roll a spring roll. Not as well as the kids could; they had natural flair and instincts and seemed to know what flavours would go together without even tasting them first. But she could do it, more or less.

And every lesson, Angus had asked her out.

She'd thought that habit would make her less susceptible to Angus. Surely she couldn't feel such a thrill every time she saw him. She'd get used to him.

Not a chance.

It was like an electric shock to see him, the air was charged and exciting when he was in the room. When she got home on Wednesday and Friday nights, her muscles were tense from controlling her actions and her head throbbed from controlling her thoughts. It was as if the past three weeks had been one long, torturous session of foreplay.

Foreplay that would never be consummated, because Elisabeth did not intend to say yes to Angus.

The bell rang, and the class filed out, eager to start their weekend. Elisabeth knew she should head straight down to the food technology room; Jennifer and Danny were always quick to get there, and now that Angus knew his way around the school he was often setting up the equipment and ingredients they needed before anyone else arrived.

Elisabeth, on the other hand, lingered for as long as she could possibly do in good conscience. She was reluctant to be in the room alone with him without the students around.

He might touch her again. Put his hands on her, draw her close to his body. And she wanted that to happen far too much to be able to risk it.

The door opened and Joanna popped her head in. 'Got a minute, or do you have to run to the gorgeous chef?'

'I've got a minute.'

Jo came in, flopped into a student chair, and pulled a chocolate bar from her pocket. 'I have some news. Danny hasn't been in detention for three and a half weeks. Ever since starting the cooking lessons.'

Elisabeth sat down hard in her own chair. 'Wow.'

'Uh huh. It's working, isn't it?' Jo knocked on a desk, decided it wasn't wood, and knocked on her head instead. 'You and Angus are doing a great job.'

Angus was doing the great job. He called every shot in that kitchen. And apparently had had an effect on the students outside it, too. She shook her head, marvelling.

'Amazing,' she said.

Jo nodded and changed the subject. 'Okay, so I know this guy who is dying to go out with you. He's Welsh. I think he's got the cutest accent. And, listen, he's a champion ballroom dancer. You'd like that, wouldn't you? He could teach you how to tango.' She put her chocolate bar between her teeth like a rose, held out her arms in a tango position and hummed a few bars of Latin-sounding music.

'A Welsh tango-dancer. Tempting, but no.' Elisabeth tidied up her desk, stacking her marking on one side.

Jo gave up on her fake dancing and unwrapped her chocolate instead. 'Okay, so if you're saying no to all my suggestions I certainly hope you're getting some good ogling time with Angus MacAllister. Has he offered to cook for you yet? Privately?'

'Yes.'

'Great! When are you getting together?'

'We're not. I said no.'

Joanna stopped, mid-bite of her chocolate, and put it down on a desk. 'Sunflower Elisabeth Read.'

Elisabeth jumped forward and clapped her hand over Jo's mouth. 'Don't you dare say my whole name out loud in school. I'd never hear the end of it if the students found out.'

Jo shook her head and Elisabeth uncovered her mouth.

'You said no to him?' Jo said. 'Are you insane? The man has two Michelin stars. And he's completely beautiful. If it were me

I'd say yes in a split second and then make sure we worked up a good appetite together first.'

'Well, I said no.' Elisabeth couldn't help giggling at Jo's shocked expression. 'I have seen his big chopper though.'

'Tell me you're not talking about a knife.'

Elisabeth shrugged. 'Sorry.'

'What else have you said no to?'

She counted off on her fingers. 'Coffee. A drink. A launch party. A weekend in the country. A movie première. *Hamlet* in Stratford.'

Jo whistled. 'All that? None of it appealed?'

'I'm not saying it didn't appeal. It's not what I want, that's all.'

'Liz, the man's rich and famous and sexy and single and he helps children. He wants to take you out and show you a great time, and you deserve it. Go out with him. Let him flatter you and feed you and make you have fun.'

'I don't want fun. I want security. I want somebody who'll always be there for me. I want children.'

At the word her eyes suddenly burned.

Oh, no. She'd decided to stop feeling bad about this.

Jo sat forward on her desk. 'Elisabeth, is this about the bab—?'

'I don't want to talk about that,' Elisabeth said firmly. 'It's finished. What matters now is that I'm looking for somebody permanent, not somebody who wants to show me a good time.'

'You mean you want to get married,' Jo said. 'You grew up with crazy hippy parents in Canada and you want a normal middle-class life.'

She felt safer now; the lump in her throat had almost gone. 'You make it sound like it's boring. But my parents never got married. There was nothing keeping them together.'

'But they did stay together. They're together still, aren't they? On that commune or wherever?'

'Yes. But I never felt safe. I never had any rules, anything to make me feel secure. I don't want—' She stopped before she said the words *my children.* 'I don't want to live like that.'

Jo was watching her carefully. 'It doesn't do you any good to keep everything inside, Elisabeth. You had a bad experience not long ago. It's okay to feel sad sometimes, and to tell your friends about it. I'm trying to make you happier.'

The expression on Jo's face made Elisabeth feel even worse. She was a good friend, and she'd do anything to help her. But honestly, truly, Elisabeth didn't need any help herself. She had everything totally under control.

See? She could even stop herself crying.

'I'm fine,' she said. 'I don't need to talk about anything. I was only trying to tell you why I don't want to go out with Angus MacAllister.' She glanced at the clock. 'And speaking of the devil, I was supposed to be with him ten minutes ago. I've got to run.'

She hugged Jo and kissed her swiftly on the cheek. 'Thank you for being concerned about me and wanting to know my problems. You're a good friend to me. And you're right, I don't appreciate you as much as I should.'

Jo picked up her chocolate bar again. 'Well, start.'

'I will.' She paused at the door, and looked over her shoulder at Joanna. She was still looking upset, despite her chocolate.

'How about you give the Welsh tango-dancer my number,' Elisabeth said.

Her friend perked up. 'Cool.'

Elisabeth smiled, glad she could make up in a small way for her shortcomings as a friend, for all the things she kept to herself.

Growing up, the atmosphere had always been so carey-sharey, everyone relating, her parents and all of the long-haired, sandalled strangers who had trooped in and out of her house, and that had all been well and good and made everybody feel better, but the problems had never got solved.

Somebody would turn up at the house with a problem, and for days they'd sleep on the couch, eat with Elisabeth and her family, hug their trees or whatever, drink her mother's home-made wine, and talk. Incessantly. About this girl who had left them, or the job they had lost, or the square landlord who had kicked them out for not paying the rent, and wasn't this a free country, man, and her parents would talk right back. The arms race. The ozone layer. Maybe they weren't being good parents. Maybe they should never have had a kid.

And they'd talk so much and so deep into the night that Elisabeth would try to read herself to sleep and couldn't. She'd hear their voices through the thin walls. Sometimes she listened because what they said was interesting, about politics or books or how to save the world. Sometimes she tried hard not to listen because what they said was something she didn't want to hear, something about her parents' own doubts and fears, about their relationship, about Elisabeth. Something that her parents should have kept out of her hearing, something they should have built boundaries around to keep her from knowing and being afraid.

Some things shouldn't be shared. Some things hurt more for being out in the open.

And the next morning her parents would tell her to pack her stuff, they were going to Manitoba to start a hemp farm, or Vancouver to join a peace rally, or somewhere else far away from the friends Elisabeth had started to make and the teachers she had started to love. Away from everything that was hers, except for her books.

She'd had her own special suitcase for her books.

At the door of the food technology room, Elisabeth shook her head. The past was over and there was no point in talking or thinking about it. Right now, she had two problem children and one problem chef to deal with.

She wondered what Angus would ask her to do with him today. And as soon as she thought it, realised she was actually looking forward to finding out.

She opened the door to a snowstorm.

White flecks sifted through the air. A fine white dust covered the work surfaces. There were drifts up to two inches deep on the floor. And Danny and Angus were both white-haired, ghost-faced, their open, laughing mouths red against their powdered skin.

As she watched Angus scooped up a handful of white stuff and flung it at Danny. It dissolved into a shower over Danny's head and shoulders.

'You're having a flour fight?' she gasped.

The two males froze. Covered in flour, they looked like ragged snowmen. Their faces were both pictures of powdered guilt.

'Danny, you know better than this,' she said. 'Miss Graham was just telling me you haven't been in trouble for over three weeks, and I was coming in here to congratulate you, and this is what I find?'

Danny shuffled his feet, kicking up small clouds. 'Angus started it.'

Elisabeth turned to Angus. 'And you. Is this the sort of thing you do in a professional kitchen? What are you teaching these kids?'

As she talked Angus's head sank lower and lower, she assumed in shame. Then she noticed that his shoulders were shaking.

'Are you laughing at me?' she asked.

He let out a great peal of laughter, doubling over and holding onto the counter for support. Danny giggled.

'It's not funny. It's going to take ages to clean this up.'

Angus collapsed backwards onto the floor, laughing, and lay there among the flour drifts.

She heard Jennifer, the traitor, stifle a giggle.

Elisabeth struggled to keep her lips from curling into a smile. Angus looked like a kid himself, a cheeky boy who'd been caught doing something wrong and knew he could charm himself out of trouble.

'You—should see—your face,' he gasped.

She put her hand in front of her mouth to hide the smile. 'At least I don't look like Casper the Friendly Ghost,' she said, and rushed out of the room.

She closed the door behind her and leaned against the wall of the corridor and laughed until tears streamed out of her eyes, trying to keep quiet so Angus and the kids wouldn't hear her through the frosted-glass door.

When she'd wiped her eyes and caught her breath and felt in control of herself again, she went back inside. Danny and Angus were on their knees on the floor sweeping up the flour into dustpans.

'See, we're being good, miss,' Angus called, smiling his beautiful wide smile. He'd cleaned the flour off his face, but it still clung to his dark hair.

'Well done,' she said, and went to stand next to Jennifer, who was lightly forking some pastry together. 'Those boys are ridiculous, aren't they?' she commented quietly to the girl, who nodded.

Elisabeth wasn't sure why Angus had started a flour fight, but she could guess. Jennifer had a small smile on her face, and Angus and Danny were chatting comfortably on the floor behind her.

Not the method she would've chosen to bond with students, but it was working.

'I can't wait till I'm a proper chef with a kitchen of my own,' Danny said. 'I'm going to have as many food fights as I want.'

'Too right, mate. Miss Read has a point, though. Once it's your kitchen you'll probably be too proud of it to want to chuck flour bombs around it. And I guess school has rules against it, too.'

'I hate school,' Danny declared.

'Don't blame you. I hated it too.'

Elisabeth, measuring out flour to Jennifer's quiet instructions, pricked up her ears. Another bonding strategy, or the truth?

'Yeah? Did you go to this school?' Danny's voice was sympathetic.

'Nah. Worse. My parents sent me to boarding-school when I was six. I went to three different prep schools and then to Emington until I was sixteen.'

'You had to live at school for ten years? That bites.'

Elisabeth glanced over at Angus. He was scrubbing flour off a worktop with a rag. He'd gone to one of the most prestigious schools in the country; no wonder he had such self-assurance, born into privilege like that. That explained the posh accent he could use when it suited him, too.

She'd visited Emington as a tourist a few years ago. It was hundreds of years old, with graceful Gothic buildings and students in formal clothing hurrying across verdant quadrangles. She remembered thinking she'd have given her eye-teeth as a child to live at school, in somewhere beautiful like that, steeped in culture and tradition and love of learning.

'It was pretty terrible,' Angus was saying. 'You couldn't ever escape it. As soon as it was legal for me to leave I went to London and got a job in a kitchen. Never looked back.'

'Yeah. I'm not going to, either.' Danny put away his dustpan and brush with a clatter and started wiping down the counter, too.

Elisabeth noticed with amusement that he was imitating the economy of Angus's movements as he cleaned.

Angus glanced up and saw Elisabeth watching them. 'What about you, Miss Read? I'll bet you loved school. I'll bet you were born with chalk and an apple in your hand.'

'I liked it,' she admitted, caught as always by his grey eyes. 'I always felt safe.'

'How do you mean, safe?'

With his attention fully on her, she hardly knew how to reply. She found herself wanting to tell him, and, because of that, she resisted. 'It just was. It was—'

'You know what people expect of you at school,' Jennifer said, just above a whisper, beside her.

She turned to stare at Jennifer. 'That's it. Exactly. So it's easy to know what to do. It's safe.'

Jennifer flushed slightly and nodded and began rolling out her pastry with fierce concentration. Elisabeth wondered what her home life was like, when school, where she was so terrified, was her safest place. She suddenly wanted to give the girl a hug.

She'd never been as scared as Jennifer. But all the same, she'd been afraid everything she loved would blow away and scatter at any moment, as fragile as autumn leaves under trees.

For the first time she noticed a small cardboard box next to Jennifer's work space. 'What have you got there?' she asked.

Jennifer dusted off her hands and opened the box with reverence. Inside rested two triangles of baklava, the golden filo pastry glistening with honey.

'Angus brought it for me,' she murmured.

'Jennifer has a sweet tooth, like me.' Angus's raspy voice was as tempting as the dessert. He appeared beside them and surveyed the pastry Jennifer was making. 'Perfect.'

Jennifer blushed furiously and smiled down at her rolling-pin.

So Angus had her in the palm of his hand, too.

'I'll be interested to see how you get on with pastry, Miss Read.' Angus reached into Elisabeth's bowl and rubbed the butter and flour between his magician's fingers. 'It's all done by touch. I think you'll be talented.'

He held her eye just a little too long, his smile just a little too wicked. And then he winked.

'Danny, mate,' he called, 'I found some perfect pears but I left them on the front seat of my car. You want to go get them for me?' He dug a set of keys out of his pocket and tossed them to Danny, who caught them mid-air and stared at them in astonishment and delight.

'It's the red Jag,' Angus added, and Danny's eyes nearly bugged out of his head. In a shot, he was out the door.

'Jennifer, would you go and help him?' Angus asked. 'Just make sure he doesn't take the car for a ride before bringing back the pears?' Jennifer nodded and trotted after Danny.

It wasn't until the door had shut behind the girl that Elisabeth realised she was alone with Angus MacAllister for the first time in three weeks. She wiped the butter and flour off her hands, and put them on her hips.

'I'm sorry,' she said.

Angus raised his eyebrows. 'Really? About what?'

'You're doing a great job with the kids. I'm sorry I doubted you.'

He half bowed in acknowledgement. 'High praise indeed from Miss Read who teaches English. Thank you, but I'll wait to accept it until I know my car is still in one piece.'

'Trust is what he needs. And feeling special is what Jennifer needs. The difference in them in three weeks is amazing.'

'And what does Elisabeth need?' He leaned against the counter next to her, his smile sexy as ever, even with his face still smudged with flour.

'Nothing.' She turned back to her bowl of dough. 'And I'm going to say no to whatever you suggest, so you might as well give up.'

'Ah, but the challenge is half the fun. Until you say yes, of course. Then we'll both start having fun.'

'Did you learn how to flirt at boarding-school? Because grown-up women don't usually fall for lines like that.'

'There weren't any women at school besides the masters' wives. Another reason I hated it there.'

She gathered the dough together into a loose ball and put it on the floured counter. 'I'm surprised you chose to volunteer your time in a school if you hated your own school days so much.'

'I didn't choose. My publicist suggested it. I'm glad she did. I never thought teaching could be so enjoyable.'

The man could make anything sound suggestive. He lit a flame under a pan of water, put a bowl into it, and started breaking squares of dark chocolate into the bowl.

It was just as she'd suspected, then: this whole thing was a bid for publicity. Angus MacAllister hadn't suddenly discovered an urge to help others.

But as she'd said, whatever his motivation, he was helping Jennifer and Danny.

'You must be having a great time teaching them how to trash a kitchen in under five minutes,' she said.

'Why did you leave the room to laugh?'

Damn. He'd figured her out.

'Because you set me up to be the bad cop,' she explained. 'If you're the jokey, rebellious one, I have to be the strict one. The kids expect it. If we let all the rules disappear, they wouldn't know how to act.'

'Ah. We work well together, don't we?'

'Yes, we do.' She said it because it was the truth. But it felt like admitting something.

'Here, do me a favour and taste this for me?'

Angus plucked a strawberry from a plate, dipped it into the bowl of chocolate and held it out to her. The deep red fruit was covered in dark melted chocolate. It was at the level of her mouth.

She looked at his face. His words had been casual, but his expression was serious except for a tiny glint of mischief in his grey eyes. He was sexy, he was dangerous, and he was fun.

And he didn't want her to taste the chocolate. He wanted her to taste him.

Her mouth was watering.

*We're at school,* she thought. *Nothing can happen. The kids will be back in a minute and it will be like this never happened. And I so, so want to.*

She leaned forward, opened her mouth, and touched the tip

of her tongue to the tip of the strawberry. She heard Angus draw in a breath.

The chocolate was warm and rich and it wasn't what she really wanted. Elisabeth leaned forward a little more and let Angus feed her the strawberry, the tips of his fingers nearly touching her lips.

The taste exploded in her mouth. The juicy soul of summer, overlaid with chocolate as sweet as temptation. Pure pleasure. Her eyes fluttered shut as she savoured the fruit, and she knew that Angus was watching her. Knew he'd wanted to give her pleasure. Knew this was part of his seduction.

Feeding her was intimate, sexual. And only a faint echo of what it would feel like to have his tongue in her mouth, his hands on her skin, his body thrusting into her.

When she opened her eyes again, the strawberry gone, she saw Angus watching her face. Close, intense, his eyes hooded, mischief replaced by desire. He'd look this way when they made love.

'You have chocolate on your mouth,' he murmured, and brushed his thumb over her lower lip. His skin was warmer than the chocolate, somehow even only the pad of his thumb strong and male. He stroked the length of her lip, and when he was finished she ran her tongue over where he had touched.

A feeling, more than a taste, and so much more delicious than any food.

He raised his thumb to his own mouth and licked the trace of chocolate off.

She moaned, deep in her throat, before she could stop herself. It was just a step away from a kiss.

For a moment, they stood there, close enough to touch, their eyes locked, their breathing shallow. Her heartbeat roared in her ears.

They had just crossed a barrier. She couldn't pretend any more that she didn't want him.

'I want a taste too,' Angus said, and he took her wrist in his clever hand. Before she could react, he guided her hand to the bowl and dipped her fingers in the warm chocolate.

He held up her hand between them so they could both see the dark molten liquid on the tips of her three middle fingers. As she watched a fat drop of chocolate slipped down the length of her index finger.

Without taking his eyes from hers, he caught the bottom of the drop with his tongue and licked, slowly, up the length of her finger. Liquid heat. Only on her finger, now, but what this would feel like on her neck...her breasts...up the inside of her thighs...

When he reached the top he gently sucked on the tip of her finger, nipping it with his smooth teeth. 'Delicious,' he said, and started on her middle finger. His tongue moving round, his lips taking small kisses.

Elisabeth watched his mouth, unhurried, thorough, and sensual. When he slipped his tongue between her fingers it was so much like him licking her between her legs she nearly lost her balance. She gripped his shoulder, and heard his small throaty sound of approval.

It took ages. It didn't take long enough. She saw the chocolate disappearing under his lips and she felt every single heartbeat as a powerful throb of desire.

And then Angus released her hand from his mouth and pulled it to his chest, bringing her body even closer. His face was only inches from hers. Near enough so his breath felt like kisses on her skin.

'Tonight,' he said, his voice a low, raspy sound that vibrated down her entire body, 'I want to take you home and taste you everywhere.' He leaned forward and touched his lips to her ear. 'Say yes, Elisabeth.'

A shiver went through her. It was exactly what she'd been thinking herself. Exactly what she wanted. To touch Angus, to experience him. She breathed in the air full of Angus MacAllister and she opened her mouth to say yes.

There was a noise at the door. Angus smoothly stepped back from her and was stirring the chocolate with a spoon when Danny burst through the door, Jennifer trailing behind.

'That is a wicked car, Angus!' he shouted, throwing a bag onto the counter and rushing up to give Angus back his keys.

'Hey, hold on, treat that fruit with respect,' protested Angus, and went to rescue the bag.

While Angus was giving the chastened Danny some lessons

on the correct handling of produce Elisabeth turned back to kneading her pastry. The pliant pastry was a poor substitute for Angus's hard body, but she craved touching something.

'You're making it tough,' Jennifer said softly beside her. 'You should handle pastry lightly.'

'Really?' Elisabeth made her voice bright and interested. 'Can you show me, Jennifer? I think this is going to end up like shoe leather.'

She listened and watched Jennifer, but she only gave her part of her attention. The other part of it was with Angus as he instructed Danny, taught the unteachable boy. He was apparently absorbed in what Danny was doing, but Elisabeth could feel the sexual tension still simmering between them although they were a room's breadth apart and each with a teenager.

Rolling of pastry, cutting of fruit, making of custard. Jennifer and Danny thought they were assembling a dessert, but Elisabeth knew better. They were building trust and self-confidence and a future. And Elisabeth and Angus were building something else, though she wasn't sure what it was yet.

He caught her eye as the tarts went into the oven, and his tongue just touched his lips. She looked away quickly.

The kids weren't the only people learning things. Angus had learned that Elisabeth wanted him, and he was apparently eager to capitalise on what he'd learned.

Elisabeth had learned that she liked Angus. Despite her suspicion of his motives; despite the fact that she'd sworn to stay away from men like him; despite the fact that the last thing she needed was temptation.

How come it was so easy to make pastry tough and so hard to make herself strong enough to resist Angus MacAllister?

Angus's and Jennifer's tarts were perfect when they came out of the oven. Danny's didn't look as good, but he'd experimented with the spices, and it tasted incredible. Elisabeth's was awful: irregular, sunken in the middle, and charred on the outside.

Elisabeth was an English teacher. She recognised a symbol when she saw one. The lesson here was: *Pay attention to your goal, and don't get distracted by sexy men who are no good for you.*

'You'll do better next time, Miss Read,' Jennifer told her.

Elisabeth glanced at Angus, who was regarding her with a twinkle and a grin, and doubted it.

As they were cleaning up Angus made a detour to stand beside her with his dishcloth. 'Thought any more about your plans for this evening, Miss Read?' he asked in a low voice. 'I'm eager to discuss the main course, after the appetisers we tasted earlier.'

'Do you always talk this way, or do I bring out the bad metaphors in you?'

'You bring out a lot in me, Elisabeth.' He subtly flicked his dishcloth in the teenagers' direction. 'So I'll pick you up at six?'

'No, thank you.' She wiped her hands on a tea towel, picked up her wonky tart, and handed it to him. 'Take this, though. In case you haven't satisfied your sweet tooth yet.'

# CHAPTER FIVE

'I WANT you to close your eyes,' said Angus, sitting on top of a table, leaning back on his hands, 'and remember the best thing you've ever eaten. I don't care it if was the fanciest, or the most expensive—I mean the best.'

From his perch on the table, he looked at the faces of the three people sitting around him on chairs. They'd closed their eyes. Danny's brow was furrowed with the intensity of his attempt to remember. Jennifer's face was slightly pinched. And Elisabeth's face, as always, was beautiful.

The most beautiful thing he'd ever seen.

And he knew it, because even though he only saw Elisabeth herself two days a week for two hours at a time, he'd seen her face in his mind for twenty-four hours of every day for the past four weeks. Working at his restaurant, travelling around London, and especially lying in his bed at night.

He hadn't been so obsessed with anything since he'd discovered that he could cook. And he hadn't been this horny since he was a teenager.

The woman was sexy as hell, even more so because she did her best not to show it. He flirted with her outrageously when the kids weren't looking and she never once flirted back. And yet the toss of her head, the sway of her hips, the firm line of her lips, the defiant sparkle in her eyes all turned him on more than any superficial flirting could do.

Except for last Friday, when he'd touched her lips, eaten

chocolate from her skin. And that had turned him on more than anything in his life had done.

Angus let his eyes settle on her face, travel over her delicate eyebrows arched over closed lids, her fine, straight nose, her satin skin. A hint of a smile passed over her lips, and he knew that she had remembered the best thing she'd ever eaten.

He hoped it had been the chocolate-dipped strawberry he'd fed her. Though there wasn't much chance of her mentioning it in front of the kids. She was as scrupulously professional in the classroom as he was in his kitchen.

'Okay, open your eyes,' he said. 'Danny, what's your best meal?'

He always started with Danny. If you didn't listen to Danny first, he just burst in anyway. The boy had a compulsive need to be noticed, a feeling that Angus recognised in himself.

There was a lot of Danny that Angus recognised in himself, as a matter of fact.

'I had this mate Azhar, right?' Danny said. 'This was when I was like ten. And one night he invited me round his for tea. His mother was the best cook ever. She had this lamb, and these lentils, and rice. I didn't know it then, but it was her spices made it taste so good. She must've ground them herself, and she used loads of coriander and that. It was just like—oh, I don't know, like every mouthful was different. I've had curries since, but never like that one.'

Elisabeth had been listening to Danny closely. 'I know Azhar,' she said. 'I didn't know you were friends.'

'Nah. We sort of stopped being mates when I came up to school here,' Danny replied, looking uncomfortable.

Angus got it. Danny's favourite food was the taste of innocence, the days when he was a kid and his friends could be any race, belong to any group. A time when he'd been allowed to express wonder.

Angus caught Elisabeth's eye and saw that she understood, too. When had he been able to communicate like this with a woman?

'What about you, Jennifer?' He leaned forward to catch her words.

'Chicken soup. With noodles. When I got a cold. My mother

used to cook a whole chicken all afternoon to make it for me. Before she died.'

Angus didn't like to push Jennifer too much; he knew the girl liked him, but he wasn't sure of her comfort zones yet, even after four weeks. But Elisabeth seemed to know how to draw the girl out.

'What was it like?' she asked.

'Deep. Golden. With some sort of green herb. The noodles were like slippery velvet.' She raised her eyes from her lap, to meet Elisabeth's. 'I only had it two or three times.'

'It must have been delicious,' Elisabeth said, and he could hear her unspoken words. *You must miss her very much.*

She was always doing this.

He'd had to work at getting the trust of these two kids. He'd had to plan what he was going to say, to put himself in their shoes and imagine how they'd react. He'd actually sat down before he'd met them and worked out a strategy based on the information that Elisabeth had given him.

But she just seemed to do it naturally. She knew how to clear a space so that people could be themselves around her. And she didn't even have to think about it first. Angus could charm people; Elisabeth could understand them.

God, he liked her. And on top of that, he liked who he was when he was with her.

Without her, he would probably have barrelled in here, given some cooking lessons, talked to the press, and forgotten about the entire thing. Because of her, he'd taken the time to get to know Danny and Jennifer. He'd thought about how he could actually help them.

And that felt good. As if some of her passion had rubbed off on him, filled up some of the emptiness he'd been feeling for so long.

'What's your favourite, Elisabeth?' he asked.

'Oatmeal cookies,' she said, and she looked so surprised at her own words that he grinned at her.

'Who made them?' he asked.

She tilted her head as she remembered. 'There was this woman who lived down the street from us when we lived in

Calgary. Her name was Miss Wood. I must have been about twelve years old and she caught me stealing her lilacs.'

'Miss!' Danny exclaimed.

Elisabeth smiled and shrugged. 'My parents believed that property was theft. I didn't think she'd miss a bunch or two. Anyway, she caught me before I could cut any. Miss Wood had a sixth sense about her flowers, I think.'

'I hope you were very ashamed of yourself,' Angus said in mock seriousness. She'd never said this much about herself before. He'd like to think it was because she'd grown more comfortable with him; he thought it was probably because she was trying to make the students more comfortable with her. But as long as he had the chance to get to know her a little better, he didn't care why.

'I was pretty embarrassed,' she admitted. 'But Miss Wood said she would give me the lilacs, if I asked her after tea. And she invited me inside.'

'For oatmeal cookies,' Angus guessed.

'First, for books. She was a retired English teacher and she was English herself. I'd never seen so many books in my life. She told me she never took tea without reading a bit of Shakespeare first. So she pulled out two copies of *As You Like It* and made me read the part about Orlando writing his love for Rosalind on all the trees of Arden forest. After that, she gave me oatmeal cookies. And Earl Grey tea.'

'She's the reason you came to England and became a teacher.'

'She was one of them. Miss Wood and her cookies and her Shakespeare. We read all the comedies and half the tragedies before I had to move again.'

With those last words, Elisabeth's smile faded, and she glanced at her watch.

Ah. Like Danny and Jennifer, Elisabeth's memories centred around loss.

Angus looked at her and wondered when he'd stopped just wanting to know what Elisabeth was like in bed and started wanting to know everything else about her, too.

'Are we going to do any cooking today?' she asked, a clear signal to change the subject.

'Eventually,' he said. 'First I want Danny and Jennifer to start designing the menus they're going to present at the competition.'

'Cool!' Danny jumped out of his chair. 'So why are we talking about it? Let's do it!'

'Calm down, mate.' Angus pushed himself forward, sat on the edge of the table. 'What we've been talking about is important. Cooking isn't just about technique and fancy ingredients. Food is memory. Food is experience. Food is emotion. So if you're creating a menu, you have to capture the right feeling. You've got to give a bit of yourself to it.'

Danny frowned. 'You want me to make curry?'

'I want you to make what you care about.'

'But I'm not even Indian.'

'Doesn't make a difference. If you put yourself into what you're doing, people will respond, whatever you're making.' Angus hopped off the table and put his hand on Danny's shoulder. 'Listen. It's easier to show you what I mean than tell you about it. That's why I've booked us a table for this Friday at Chanticleer.'

He was looking straight at Elisabeth when he said it, so he saw her blinking in shock.

'Chanticleer?' she said. 'Isn't that supposed to be one of the most expensive restaurants in London?'

He grinned at her. 'It's also one of the best. The chef is my friend Damien Virata.'

'But Danny and Jennifer—'

'Won't have to pay for a thing. Neither will you. It's my treat.'

'But—'

'I can afford it, if that's what you're worried about.'

'No, that's not—it's just that—'

He loved seeing the teacher lost for words.

'I've discussed it with Joanna Graham, and she agreed that experiencing innovative cuisine would enhance Jennifer and Danny's learning. She's got permission from their parents already. Provided, of course, that you come as well.'

Elisabeth looked stunned.

Finally, after four weeks of trying, he'd hit upon an invitation that she couldn't refuse.

'I've booked the table for six o'clock. The place shouldn't be full at that hour. Miss Graham said she'd give you all a ride there in her car. We should be done by eight o'clock, nine at the latest. Just in case you have other plans,' he added, looking significantly at Elisabeth.

She was shaking her head, but it wasn't in refusal. 'Mr MacAllister, I believe you are the most stubborn man in existence,' she said.

'Why thank you, Miss Read,' he replied.

The package was waiting for her on her doorstep when she got home from school on Friday afternoon. Elisabeth recognised her mother's slanted handwriting on the address label right away.

It wasn't even close to her birthday, but her parents had never been very organised about remembering dates. If her parents saw a gift for her, they'd send it. When she was a kid she'd rarely had a party on her actual birthday. They'd throw her parties at other times, mostly to surprise her, so she hadn't really missed out on anything except for the pleasure of anticipation, and of inviting her friends herself. Then again, she hadn't had much time to make friends before her family had moved on again.

She made herself a cup of tea and sat down with the package and the telephone, dialling her parents' number. Her mother picked up the phone on the first ring.

'Hey, Poppy,' Elisabeth greeted her. 'How are you?'

'Sunny! Great. Have you got it? Open it.'

She should have known her mother would be haunting the phone, waiting for Elisabeth to receive the package and call. She loved knowing what Elisabeth's reaction was when she opened a present. Elisabeth smiled, feeling warmth at Poppy's enthusiasm. She loved this aspect of her mother's childlikeness, this eager generosity.

She began to unwrap the package.

'You're pulling it open carefully, aren't you?' her mother said. 'Keeping the paper all in one piece?'

'Yes.' She unfolded one end and giggled at how well her mother knew her.

'Just rip it. Quick. I can't wait. You are going to love this.'

She wondered. Her mother and she didn't share many tastes. If she hadn't looked so much like her parents, she'd have spent even more of her childhood wondering if she was really related to them. She kept the wrapping paper intact, but she opened it more quickly. There was a long cardboard box inside.

'Is it open yet?'

'I'm lifting the lid now.' She pulled it off, and she gasped.

'You love it, don't you? Take it out. Tell me.'

Elisabeth lifted a long chain of glass beads. Each bead was its own intense shade of green, its own unique shape. Like light shining through leaves of all the kinds of trees in a forest.

It was one of the tastes that she and her mother did share—a love of beautiful, unusual jewellery. She had many pieces her mother had given her, all of them more precious than their actual value. This one reminded her of some of the places where they'd lived in Canada. Quiet, living beauty.

'It's gorgeous.'

Her mother sighed in pleasure. 'You don't have enough wilderness there in England. You need a little to keep with you. Something wild-coloured.'

'It reminds me of trees. I love it, Mom.'

At the last word, Poppy sighed in a different way. 'I used to hate you calling me that. I like it now. Is that freaky?'

'Well, you are my mother.' Elisabeth tried on the necklace, felt its cool, smooth weight.

'Yeah. I wonder more and more these days whether I acted like one, though, babe. I treated you like a friend, and maybe you needed a parent. We were trying to start a new world, you know? No hierarchies, no obligations. But you turned out okay. You're helping people. We're proud of you.'

Yes, her teaching was like her parents' quest to save the world, she supposed. She didn't have to fling herself in front of bulldozers or chain herself to trucks carrying nuclear missiles, but it felt as important. Especially these days, working with Jennifer and Danny and Angus. It was safer physically, but no less emotionally dangerous.

'I got it from you,' she said, and for the first time really knew it was true. Her crazy upbringing had given her something other than insecurities and wild desires and a need for safety. It had given her something precious.

'Yeah. You're doing good, babe. You'll be a good mother too, when it happens for you again. Better than me.'

She stroked the beads of the necklace to distract her from what her mother was saying. She thought of Poppy's simple joy at giving a gift. So many of Poppy's joys were simple. It would be so tempting to live that way for once, to give up seeing the implications of everything and just be.

She'd tried to do that with Robin. She was a lot like her parents in several ways, it seemed. The successes, and the failures.

And yet having her mother admit her failures let Elisabeth see them in a wider perspective, as an outsider might have. As one of her own teachers might have, if they had asked a question like the one Angus had asked on Wednesday, about food and emotion.

She'd been a lonely girl, always moving, always insecure. But she'd had her books, and had parents who felt great joy whenever they could make her happy. It was more than many children ever had.

'You both loved me,' she said. 'That's what counts.'

Saying that, too, she knew it was true.


'Joanna, would you please slow down?'

'What?' Jo reached over and turned down the radio, causing the car to swerve to the left.

'Slow down. There are children in the car.'

'They're teenagers. Teenagers love to go fast. Don't you, teenagers?'

'Yes, miss,' came Danny's voice from where he and Jennifer were crammed into the tiny seats in the back of the convertible.

'See?' Jo's hand stretched towards the radio again, but Elisabeth beat her to it. She switched the balance so that the sound was all transferred to the speakers in the back, and then turned the volume up.

Jo smiled, recognising the classic ploy of distracting students with something loud so you could get in a private conversation. 'I thought you'd be impatient to get there, seeing as who's hosting the evening.'

'I've turned down half a dozen dates with Angus MacAllister in the past month. What makes you think I'm eager to see him tonight?'

'Dress. Heels. Necklace. Lipstick.' Jo took a corner at speed. 'You look fantastic.'

'It's an expensive restaurant.' But Elisabeth knew that wasn't why she'd dressed up in her smallest little black dress and her highest little black heels.

She'd dressed this way out of anticipation and simple joy.

But she wasn't going to admit that.

Jo sank her voice. 'If he asks you home tonight after dinner, I'll cover for you with the kids. Don't worry about it.'

'I told you. Angus MacAllister is everything I don't need.'

'Believe me, I say that about chocolate every day. Sometimes we have to go for what we want instead of what we need.' She stopped at a red light. 'And, Elisabeth, you know you don't fool me, darling. You love going fast in this car just as much as I do.'

'I don't.'

The light turned green, and Jo put her foot down. The convertible leapt forward with a roar and a screech of tyres. Elisabeth was flung backwards into her seat and she heard Jennifer yelp.

'How'd you like that?' Joanna cried, her foot still on the accelerator, the car going faster every second.

'I—'

'Heart beating fast? Feel like you're really alive?'

Elisabeth put her hand on her chest. Her heart was hammering and her body was thrumming with adrenaline.

She laughed. 'Yes. I do.'

'Knew it.'

Jo sounded so pleased with herself that Elisabeth laughed again. 'All right. I'll tell you my deepest, darkest secret. I'm looking forward to spending an evening with Angus MacAllister.'

'Ha!' Jo thumped the steering wheel in triumph.

'But nothing's going to happen. The kids will be there the whole time.'

'I wouldn't count on it. Angus MacAllister looks like a man who'll do anything to get what he wants.' Jo pulled up to the kerb and switched off the radio. 'Here we are, kids!'

Elisabeth's dress rode up as she climbed out of the convertible and she felt the cool spring air on her bare legs and arms. Aside from her jewellery, she was normally a conservative dresser; years of cheesecloth and patchwork hand-me-downs had instilled a love of simple, well-tailored clothes. But she'd thought of Angus when she'd chosen her dress, a sleeveless clingy sheath that ended several inches above her knee. And her heels were slim-strapped, open-toed, practically pornographic.

She didn't feel like Miss Elisabeth Read, maiden teacher. She felt like an attractive woman about to have a date with a sexy man. And Jo's comment about Angus being the type to do anything to get what he wanted sent Elisabeth's heart racing faster than the speeding car had done.

But, shoes and dress aside, this was a safe date. Nothing was going to happen, and she could relax and enjoy it.

She remembered when she'd last thought that; when Angus had sent the children away and they'd been alone together. Something had happened then, all right.

She curled her fingers around the green-glass necklace, a reminder of the conversation she'd had with her mother that afternoon. And of her parents' philosophy, echoed in a hundred sixties' songs.

*Be here now.*

Elisabeth knew the bad side of that hippy-wisdom. If you never thought of the future, you were the victim of every passing impulse.

But talking with her mother had made her see that philosophy had its place. It could make you stop and enjoy the present. And it could give you courage to do what you wanted to.

She thought about what had happened on Wednesday—how Angus had coaxed her into revealing something about her past. It had felt good.

She was glad he'd tricked her into coming out with him.

She checked out Chanticleer's façade. She'd read about the place in magazine reviews, all raving about the most innovative cuisine in Great Britain, but she'd never expected to come here herself. The outside was unprepossessing: plain brick, Georgian, with tall sashed windows that were frosted halfway down their length. There was no sign, just a life-sized brass rooster statue on a waist-height pillar near the front door.

Now *that* was pretentious, Elisabeth thought. Not even putting the restaurant's name outside, and expecting the clientele to remember that Chanticleer was the name of a folk-tale rooster, retold in the *Canterbury Tales*.

Still, at least it continued the chicken theme that Angus had introduced the first time she'd met him. She wondered if Angus was issuing a sort of challenge to her again, and she smiled.

'Do you think it's dead fancy, miss?' Danny asked at her elbow.

Danny, the braggart, sounded frightened. These kids had probably never been in a restaurant more sophisticated than their local Chinese take-away. They were bound to be more daunted than she was.

She winked at Danny. She wasn't convinced he was going to behave himself, but she was going to give him all the trust she could, regardless.

'Tell you what,' she said. 'I think we should use the wrong fork just to see what happens.'

'Yeah, I dare you.'

She put her hand on Jennifer's shoulder. The girl was tense. 'You'll have to sit next to me, just in case Angus and Danny start talking football again. Otherwise I might fall asleep in my soup.'

They walked up the staircase together and as they passed the bronze rooster Elisabeth patted it on its head. She wasn't going to be chicken. She intended to enjoy every moment of this evening.

As soon as they stepped through the doorway a man wearing a suit that was probably more expensive than Elisabeth's entire wardrobe greeted them. 'Miss Read? Mr MacAllister is waiting for you at your table.'

The restaurant was bright, decorated in cream and warm

orange, but she stopped noticing it as soon as she recognised the comfortable slouch of a dark-suited figure at a table in the corner.

Angus stood when they approached. He was wearing a chocolate-coloured suit, perfectly tailored to his body, with a snow-white shirt open at the throat. A lock of his dark brown hair fell over his forehead. Occasionally over the past four weeks he'd had a shadow of stubble on his face, but tonight he was clean-shaven, emphasising the line of his jaw and the dimple in his chin.

Elisabeth stared. He was the best-looking man she had ever seen.

The entire restaurant, the tables, the flowers, the tasteful lamps, the two teenagers standing beside her, all vanished. His gaze started at her face, and took in her dress, her bare arms, her legs, her silly sexy shoes.

It only took a few seconds, and during that whole time it felt as if his ravaged, sensitive hands were trailing up and down her body. For a fleeting moment, Elisabeth saw such longing in his eyes that she could not breathe.

Then he grinned. 'I'm excited that you're here.'

For the first time in her life, Elisabeth was annoyed the English language only had one second person pronoun, so she couldn't tell whether Angus was talking just to her, or to all three of them. Then she mentally shook herself. It didn't matter.

She was excited she was here, too.

He pulled out a suede-upholstered chair for her and she sank into it and watched him do the same thing for Jennifer, gesturing Danny into the seat to his right, making sure they both had glasses of mineral water. His body was full of energy.

'I envy you three so much,' he said. 'You're about to have an experience like nothing else you've had before. Damien Virata is the most extraordinary chef working in Britain today. You've got to leave all your preconceptions behind, and rely on your senses only. Look, and smell, and feel, and taste. Don't think.'

He sat beside Elisabeth and held out a champagne flute to her. She took it, her fingers brushing his. She felt the contrast between the chilled glass and his warm flesh.

'Thank you for letting me do this,' he said to her. 'I've been looking forward to it for days.'

And with that, Elisabeth realised that the impreciseness of the English language really didn't matter, because she liked Angus all the more for wanting to take her out, and being generous enough to share the experience with others.

'Cheers.' She chimed her glass with his, then with the kids' glasses of sparkling water, and took a sip. On her tongue, platinum bubbles; around her body, buttery suede; in the air, electricity.

Her senses seemed preternaturally sharpened from being close to Angus without the possibility of moving away. She could practically feel the soft texture of his suit by looking at it. Even though she couldn't see underneath the table, she knew from a tingle on the side of her right knee that his own knee was inches from hers.

'I let Damien choose our menu,' Angus said. 'Jennifer, you scrub up well, don't you? That's a pretty dress.'

Elisabeth tore her eyes away from Angus's left hand, lying on the tablecloth very close to her right hand, to look at her students. Jennifer wore a sky-blue dress with a white cardigan over it. Out of her uniform she looked older, much less like a frightened little girl. She blushed furiously at Angus's compliment.

*She has a crush on Angus,* Elisabeth realised, and smiled. She really couldn't blame her.

Danny was wearing his school shirt, tucked in for once, and a blue tie. It was loose around his neck, but at least it wasn't trailing out of his pocket.

Elisabeth, influenced by the surroundings and her own sensory overload, saw the four of them briefly as an outsider might: a smart teenage boy, thrilled by where he was; a young girl on the threshold of adulthood; a happy, handsome man, courteous and attentive; and a woman dressed to the nines, enjoying herself.

It was a picture she would have considered impossible only days before.

A plate appeared before her, interrupting her reverie. She blinked down at the white porcelain overlaid with pink and green slivers, laced with yellow sauce.

'This looks more like art than food,' she said. 'What is it?'

Angus's eyes sparkled. 'Not telling. Just try it.'

She took a forkful: some silky texture, with a crispy edge, a sweetness overlaid with something intensely salty. It was fish, but she didn't have a clue what else was on the plate. The flavours melded together, one and then the other dominating on her palate.

Elisabeth glanced at the teenagers, and she could see what her own expression was probably like, mirrored in their faces. Bafflement, and wonder, and a surprised pleasure.

'Do you like it?' Angus leaned forward, watching her.

'It's not like anything else I've ever tasted.'

'Yes, but do you like it?'

She took another bite, considered.

'Yes.'

Angus clapped his hands together and rubbed them in joy. His smile bathed his face in light.

It was funny—Danny and Jennifer appeared older in these surroundings, but Angus was so full of excitement that he seemed almost like a boy.

She thought of her mother, waiting breathlessly as Elisabeth opened her present.

'Absolutely brilliant,' he said.

That course was followed by a frothy green palate- cleansing drink, and then by another course, and another. All of them were small, but the balance of textures and flavours was constantly surprising.

Elisabeth knew nothing about food. She'd been raised on a diet of lentils and strange herbal teas. But even she could appreciate the barrage of sensory detail. Her mouth and tongue had never been so subtly seduced.

And the rest of her body inevitably followed.

Angus sat so close to her. His throaty voice laughing, explaining aspects of the dishes to the students in the way that she would analyse a poem. His hand lingering on her wrist as he asked her a question.

She caught every nuance of his expression, felt the power of his delight. The touch of his eyes crackled on her skin. His intimate questions, almost-whispered comments, tantalised her ears.

Every time she took a bite, she felt her rationality slipping away.

'Here,' he said to her, 'you can't eat each part separately, it's got to go together, the fruit and the lamb and the purée and the sauce. Try it like this.' Angus held a fork out to her, balanced with the different parts of the dish together.

Without thinking, she stretched her neck forward, opened her mouth for Angus to feed her. She saw his grey eyes focused on her mouth as she closed her lips around his fork.

'Are you enjoying it?' A deep, rich voice came from behind her. Elisabeth, startled, pulled away from Angus and looked around.

The man was short and stocky, with dark curly hair. He wore a chef's white tunic and chequered trousers.

'Damien!' Angus was out of his chair and shaking the chef's hand. 'Fantastic grub, as always.'

The famous chef beamed at all of them, his cheeks rosy and shiny. 'I'm glad to have the next generation here. Would you like to see the kitchen before dessert?'

Jennifer's wide eyes and Danny's 'I'm cool' shrug were answer enough.

As they walked into the kitchen Angus's hand rested in the small of Elisabeth's back, creating a pool of heat that spread through her body. Still, it was a shock to encounter the steam of Chanticleer's kitchen, full of people and noise and flames. Was this loud, frantic, dangerous place the place where Angus felt at home?

She saw, but couldn't hear, Damien speaking with Jennifer and Danny and pointing out different areas of the kitchen. Angus's hand closed around Elisabeth's wrist.

'Come here,' he murmured in her ear, tugging her gently to one side.

He opened a steel door in the wall and pulled her in after him. She saw shelves stacked with produce and plastic boxes. She felt the whisper of a chill and realised that they were in a walk-in refrigerator.

Angus shut the door after them.

# CHAPTER SIX

ANGUS leaned back against the door, his bright smile on his face, looking irresistible and dangerous.

'I've been dying to get you alone,' he said.

She rubbed her hands along her bare arms, though she wasn't cold yet. 'In a refrigerator?'

'Elisabeth, I'd be warm in a freezer if you were there.' He looked her up and down again, as he had when she'd first arrived, and Elisabeth shivered. Not from the cold this time, either. 'You are stunning. It's taken all my will-power to keep my hands off you tonight.'

*Likewise,* Elisabeth thought, but she only rubbed her arms again.

He stepped away from the door, closer to her, and held his hands above her bare shoulders. Not touching, but Elisabeth could feel his heat.

'I'd love to warm you up,' he said. 'May I?'

*Please, please, please, yes.* Elisabeth bit her lip. 'The children—'

'Will be fine for the next twenty minutes, at least. They won't miss us, but this place could feel very cold if we don't build up some body heat soon.'

'You could let us out.' Her voice sounded unconvincing even to her. Maybe it was because she couldn't quite catch her breath.

Angus shook his head. 'Not a chance, Miss Read. You've been dodging me since the day you met me, and I want to know why. At first I thought it was because you were angry with me.

But I don't think that's true any more. Now I think it's because you don't trust me. Is that right?'

She raised her eyebrows and crossed her arms more tightly on her chest. 'And I'm supposed to trust somebody who traps me in a refrigerator?'

'You can leave whenever you want to. Just hit the button on the door.' But he didn't move away from her, and she didn't move either.

'Why don't you trust me?' he asked.

'Because you're a flirt and you charm people without even thinking. You don't mean it.'

'Now, there you're wrong, Elisabeth. I think about it a lot.' A fine mist of condensation hung in his words, and in her breath between them. 'And I genuinely want to help Danny and Jennifer, if that's what you're worried about. I'm not using them. I'm not using you.'

'I'm more worried that you've flirted with me from the moment you met me and you've been trying to get me into bed with you for nearly as long. It's something you do with a lot of women, so I've heard.'

He nodded. 'Ah. So it's my public image you don't like. Well, that makes sense. But I wouldn't believe everything you read in the newspapers.'

'So you don't have a different woman in your bed every week?'

'I know a lot of women and I go on dates with some of them occasionally. But, no, I don't usually sleep with them. And not one of the women I know makes me feel the way that you do.'

Angus hadn't moved since he'd approached her; his hands still hovered over her shoulders. She was starting to feel the cold on the backs of her bare legs, but everywhere that was near Angus was almost too hot to bear.

'How do I make you feel?' she asked.

'Alive. Intrigued. Hungry.' His mouth quirked up on one side. 'Horny.'

'Likewise.' This time, she did say it. It slipped out before she could stop herself.

His smile, like a hundred-watt bulb. He had white teeth, slightly crooked on the bottom, a small imperfection that made him even more perfect. His lips were well formed, soft and yet masculine.

But it wasn't his lips and teeth that made his smile so dazzling. It was the ardency behind it, the enthusiasm, the joy in being.

The way Elisabeth felt right now.

'I won't touch you unless you want me to,' Angus said. 'Do you?'

'Yes.'

He stared into her eyes for a moment, as if he couldn't quite believe what she'd said. Not surprising, as she could hardly believe it herself.

Then his smile faded, his expression became intent. His hands still didn't touch her. He bit his lip, as if he were concentrating hard. A line appeared between his eyebrows.

He inhaled once, deeply, and then let his hands drop down onto her bare shoulders.

They both held their breaths. Elisabeth closed her eyes to savour the feeling of his hands on her skin, and then opened them again because she didn't want to miss a single instant of seeing him.

Slowly he slid his palms down the length of her arms. She could feel every hair raise itself into goose-bumps.

Their hands met, and their fingers twined together.

Elisabeth, with some far-flung rational corner of her brain, marvelled at herself. She was standing close to Angus MacAllister, holding his hands, looking frankly into his face. In a refrigerator. Where someone could come in any minute, looking for tomatoes or something.

And it felt wonderful.

Despite her high heels, he was still taller than her. She stood on her toes, stretched up her face, and met his mouth as he leaned down to her.

His lips were warmer than she would have imagined in this cold room. Gentle, and sweet, and lingering. He felt wholly other to her, totally masculine, unlike anything she'd felt before. And yet familiar, as if she'd been waiting for him.

Time passed, the two of them with hands linked, lips pressed together. Not exploring, not moving—just touching, this first time.

When they broke apart Elisabeth felt as if her eyes were shining.

Their kiss had been innocent and romantic. Like the kiss in a fairy tale that woke up the sleeping princess. And she felt awake, aware, buzzing with the possibilities of the present.

Angus swallowed. 'Wow,' he said.

'Wow,' she said back.

'I've been waiting to kiss you for a while. But I didn't expect—'

'I thought it would be—' She thought of the word. Not sexier, because it had been the sexiest thing she'd ever experienced. 'More carnal.'

He nodded. 'I feel like I should recite some poetry or something.' He brought her hands up to his chest and stroked the backs of them with his thumbs.

'If you're having urges to recite poetry, I think you'd better kiss me again.'

She lifted her hands from his and buried them in his glossy hair. Angus curled his fingers around her hips, pulled her closer.

And she knew that their kiss hadn't been innocent at all, because this close she could feel the hard ridge of his erection through their clothes.

White-hot desire rushed through her and she pulled his head down and kissed Angus as if she wanted to devour him.

Firm lips, hard, smooth teeth, just crooked on the bottom. Rough tongue, the satin of inside his mouth.

Angus groaned and lifted her so that she was still closer to him, her toes barely touching the floor. And then his hands were sliding up her back, down over her bottom, burning fingerprints on her even through her clothes.

Touching his hair wasn't enough. Elisabeth put her hands on his shoulders, as she'd been dying to, stroked the soft material of his suit. Down his arms and to his hips.

His mouth was wonderful. Their kisses were fierce and desperate. And with him holding her like this, Elisabeth could feel every inch of his body against her, as lithe and strong as she'd thought it would be.

They were going to get caught any minute. But she needed

more. She let her hand fall to the curve of his backside and dug her fingers into his firm flesh. Angus made a rough sound in his throat, pulled up her leg around his hip, and she felt him pushing even harder against her. With her thigh lifted around him, her dress riding up, her sex rubbed intimately against his erection.

They were in a refrigerator, and she felt as if she were burning up.

When they broke apart, their breaths came in jagged clouds.

'Now *that* was carnal,' she gasped.

'I was turned on by romantic, too.' He dropped another kiss on her lips, touched his tongue to hers briefly before parting to look in her eyes again.

'I noticed,' she said, letting her gaze fall to where their crotches were glued together.

He let his hand creep underneath the hem of her skirt, rest on the back of her thigh.

'Trust me yet?' he said.

'No.' She couldn't resist nipping at his bottom lip.

His smile. 'We should probably get out of here before the kids finish their tour.'

Oh. She'd forgotten about Danny and Jennifer.

With an even greater sense of shock, she realised that this had probably been the longest she hadn't thought about the kids she taught in months.

Elisabeth put both her feet on the floor, but she kept her hands on his waist. He kissed her on the cheek this time, and on her forehead. Each kiss cooled quickly in the chilled air.

'We've only got dessert to get through. And that won't take long. When is your friend picking them up?'

She had to stop touching him with one hand, but she checked her watch anyway. Quarter past eight. 'In fifteen minutes.'

'Brilliant. You'll come back to my house with me.'

It was a statement, not a question. Punctuated with more kisses. And it was an arrogant thing to say, something a celebrity would say, someone who expected to get women with a crook of his finger.

Except when she didn't reply he stopped pressing his lips to her temple and looked her in the face. His forehead was creased and his grey eyes seemed almost pained.

'You will, won't you, Elisabeth? You do trust me a little, don't you?'

His raspy voice held something she hadn't quite heard there before. Something she was sure she'd heard in her own voice before, once upon a time. An earnestness she'd felt, and couldn't believe that he could feel.

'For a night?' she said lightly. 'That's not a whole lot of trust.'

He caught her hands in his again. 'Stay for a night. Stay for a week. I want to get to know you, in every way I can.'

His words promised pleasure. She thought about the biblical sense of the word 'know'. 'I'd like to know you too,' she said.

He exhaled in a long rush, and kissed her lips. 'Okay. You go ahead out and I'll join you at the table. I think I'd better stay in here for a minute or two to calm down.'

Now that she wasn't pressed against him, she could see that the line of his erection was clearly visible in his trousers.

Another wave of desire swept through her. She swallowed, hesitating, hating to leave him even for a moment.

He stroked down her back, once more. 'Go. And, Elisabeth…?'

'Mmm?' She wiped a trace of lipstick from his bottom lip with her thumb, and wanted to put it back there all over again.

'Try to trust me. For tonight, at least.'

He looked as serious and as earnest as he had during that first lesson, when he'd shown them his hands and his scars. She remembered him throwing Danny his car keys.

She nodded and pushed open the refrigerator door.

As soon as she was gone, Angus let out the breath he'd been holding in a long stream of condensation, and leaned back against a shelf of lettuce.

She'd nodded. She was going to try to trust him.

And the reason he was leaning against lettuce, his legs barely able to hold his body up, was partly because he was more turned on than he had been in his entire life, just from kissing Elisabeth and touching, briefly, her naked skin.

But that was only part of it. The other part was an overwhelming, heart-thumping feeling of relief.

He'd planned the evening to be one of subtle seduction. Nothing too overt, just little touches, lingering glances, stuff that would fall below the students' radar. And then an invitation for coffee at the end of the evening, a chance to talk with Elisabeth and spend some time with her.

Then she'd shown up in that dress, and the 'subtle' plans had gone out the window.

Elisabeth Read in a little black dress was more temptation than any rational man could take.

As soon as he'd seen her in that dress, demure and incredibly sexy, he'd known he would never be satisfied with coffee and conversation. Like the moment when he'd touched her lips with his finger, flirtation had suddenly become need. If he hadn't dragged her into this refrigerator, he would have spontaneously combusted from pure frustration at not being able to touch her.

And yet touching hadn't been enough. As soon as they'd been alone, he'd discovered that he needed more.

Angus's breathing gradually slowed and he stood up straight, brushing down his suit and rearranging the collar of his shirt.

What was going on with him? Since when had he begged a woman for anything, let alone her trust?

He already had Elisabeth's admiration and her desire. She followed his lead in the kitchen, and worked well with him with the kids. He was even, after a very shaky start, reasonably sure of her friendship. He'd worked hard to gain all of that with her. And that was, normally, enough for him.

But instead he'd wanted her to know everything he felt. He wanted her to trust him with her body and with her emotions, too. If only for one night.

He wiped his mouth with the back of his hand and saw, with a smile, that Elisabeth had missed some of her lipstick.

Angus thought about Elisabeth's mouth. Throwing back one of her tart comments. Pressing itself together, trying to resist smiling. Twitching at the corners with humour. And kissing him so passionately and gently, and then so passionately and strong.

He didn't know what was happening to him, why he felt differently about her than any other woman he'd ever known.

The breast pocket of his suit buzzed, and in an automatic movement, his mind still on Elisabeth's mouth, he flipped out his mobile phone and pressed the 'answer' button.

'MacAllister.'

'Angus, good news. I've set you up the interviews about your school charity work. I've got the *Journal* and the *Herald* on board and someone's coming over from the *New York Press* next week to—'

His publicist. 'Christine, I'm in a refrigerator and I'm busy. Call me tomorrow.'

He took the phone away from his ear and pressed the 'power off' button.

Then he looked at the dead state-of-the-art mobile phone in his hand, realising what he'd just done.

He'd never turned off this phone before. Or the phone he'd had before this one, or the one he'd had before that. Or any phone he'd ever owned in his life.

He'd known logically that they had 'off' buttons. But he'd never pressed one. He'd needed to stay available every minute of the day, in case there was an emergency at his restaurant, in case somebody needed him, in case there was a publicity opportunity he had to take advantage of.

Tonight, he'd broken the habit of his entire adult life without even thinking about it because Elisabeth Read was more important than any phone call he could ever get.

Angus replaced his phone in his pocket, checked his suit again for wrinkles, looked at his reflection in the steel door to check for any stray lipstick marks, and grinned at himself.

He didn't know what was going on, and he didn't know what was going to happen. But he was looking forward to finding out.

From a cold, hot, quiet intimacy to a room full of clangs, shouts, steam, sizzles. Elisabeth felt as if she'd stepped into a different world.

But it wasn't the world that had changed. It was her.

She spotted Jennifer, Danny and Damien, and she touched her green glass necklace as she dodged her way across the kitchen.

*Be here now.*

*Try to trust me. For tonight, at least.*

Same message.

The teenagers were so absorbed in what Damien was telling them that they didn't glance in her direction when she joined them, and she guessed they'd hardly registered her and Angus's absence. Damien made no comment either.

She wondered if Angus had set up this whole thing with Damien, had planned on getting her alone in the refrigerator. But then she pushed the thought aside. She'd promised to trust him, she reminded herself.

Plus, she rather liked the idea that Angus had gone to elaborate lengths to find a way to touch her in private. Like their first kiss, it was romantic. And for most of her life, Elisabeth had only found romance in books.

The dining room was another world again: calm, hushed, welcoming. The candles and the orange walls made her feel like Cinderella in her pumpkin carriage riding toward her one magical night.

Danny had been as silent as Jennifer with Damien but as soon as the chef left them at the door of the dining room he erupted into speech. 'Oh, my God, that was so wicked, did you see what they were doing with the blow torch, I wanna use one of those I'm gonna ask Angus, and did you see that thing they were doing with *hay* I mean can you believe it old dried-out grass, and did you see when that guy poured in the brandy and it like exploded in the pan, I want to do that in the contest, like *boom* and then it sort of melts into a sauce, d'you think they would let me do that, miss? And—'

'Were you impressed by anything except the explosions, mate?' Angus slipped into his seat beside them, his voice amused, his appearance unruffled. Elisabeth, who had thought she'd calmed down a little, throbbed and felt her breasts tighten. His knee touched hers under the table.

As soon as Angus appeared the dessert did, too, borne by

waiters as silent as ghosts. 'I love this one,' Angus said to all of them. The white plates each held five little white pots. 'Damien made it for me because I'm an ice-cream fiend. Taste them all and try to guess the flavours.'

The spoon she'd been given was tiny, a slender curve of silver, and Elisabeth thought that her hands were still too unsteady to handle it gracefully. She watched the other three try their desserts. Jennifer and Danny were concentrating fiercely. Angus, the teensy silver spoon balanced in his sensitive fingers, had an expression of pure pleasure on his face as he ate.

It was nearly the same expression he'd had when he'd touched her for the first time. After he'd kissed her. Elisabeth swallowed.

She wondered if she'd ever watch him eating anything again without thinking of that.

Jennifer and Danny guessed the flavours; she barely heard them. Angus turned to Elisabeth. 'You should try it. We've only got ten minutes left.' He winked almost imperceptibly.

He was so cocky, and her first response was the self-defensive one. *I haven't agreed to come home with you yet.* But it wouldn't be true. She'd decided to trust him and part of that was trusting her feelings about him.

She'd agreed to go home with him already.

She picked up her spoon, tried her dessert, tasted five types of ice cream and Angus. There was a flavour that wasn't on her plate: tasted on his lips, the air electric, heart hammering with desire and the danger of being caught.

Angus reached underneath the table, ran a swift touch up the outside of her thigh, and she knew he was thinking the same thing.

It was the slowest and the fastest ten minutes of her life. If she'd thought she'd been hyperaware during dinner, she was twenty times more so now. Every second was full of sensations and emotions, every bit of it saturated with the thought, *I'm going to spend the night with Angus.*

He checked his watch and his surprise at the time was so exaggerated to Elisabeth's eyes that she had to stifle a laugh. 'Is it that late? Kids, Miss Graham is going to be waiting for you outside. Come on, I'll take you out to see if she's there.' He stood and pretended to inspect Elisabeth's plate. 'Why don't you finish your dessert, Elisabeth, and I'll get a taxi for you afterwards?'

Smooth operator. She said goodbye to Jennifer and Danny. The girl was smiling, the boy was still running over with chatter she could hear all the way out of the restaurant.

And then she was alone at the table with three empty seats, five styles of ice cream, and her own thoughts.

What on earth was she doing?

This wasn't like a date. This wasn't meeting a man, doing something together, getting to know each other better to see if they wanted to embark upon a relationship.

This was going home with a man she barely knew to have sex with him.

This wasn't *Be here now*. It was *Be here stupid*.

Elisabeth stood up and pushed her chair back.

'Don't even think of running away.' Angus's arm was around her shoulders, his voice in her ear. He pressed a kiss to her temple and Elisabeth breathed in his lemony, masculine scent.

'I don't think this is a good idea,' she said.

'I think it's a very good idea indeed,' he replied. 'How about we get in a taxi back to my place and debate it on the way?'

'We don't need to debate.'

'Great. Let's go home, then.' He kissed the hollow beneath her ear and a shiver went down Elisabeth's spine. 'Or are you trying to tell me you've chickened out?'

The word hit in exactly the right place. She turned, out of his arms, and faced him. 'You and your bloody chickens—'

Angus threw back his head and laughed. 'I love that strict-teacher act of yours. I think it's sexy as hell.'

Angus laughing was sexy as hell. And she felt herself rising to his challenge, as always. 'It's not an act, and you're trying to wind me up so I'll agree to come home with you just to prove you wrong.'

'That is precisely the idea, Miss Read.'

His face was irrepressible, full of glee and life and clever mischief.

'Come on, Elisabeth,' he said, and he took her hand in his again. 'Come home and play with me.'

*Play.*

He'd hit on the right word again. The one word that grabbed her by the gut and filled her with so much longing that she could barely keep from throwing herself at him.

It was playing. It was a game, something for fun. As she hadn't had in years. Something that didn't matter, that was just for her, a treat better than any dessert.

If this was play, she didn't need to worry. She could keep control. She could trust Angus for the length of a game.

Games didn't require you to give your heart.

'Right,' she said. 'Let's go before I change my mind. But if you haven't won the debate by the end of the taxi ride, I'm going home.'

She turned and headed for the door, feeling him follow her, enjoying playing the role of sexy teacher now that it was all a game.

Only after she'd covered the length of the restaurant, straight-spined, and thanked the *maître d'* and gone out the door and onto the pavement, did she look at Angus. He was right behind her, wide-eyed, biting his lip, looking like a man entranced.

'My God, you know how to turn me on,' he said, and raised his arm for a taxi.

A black cab glided to a halt in front of them and they climbed in. She could feel Angus close to her as she slid across the seat. He gave the driver an address and sat down close beside her, his thigh pressing the length of hers.

'I was on the junior debate team at school,' he said.

'Good, then you know how to follow the rules,' she said smoothly, wriggling just slightly away so she was no longer touching him. 'You state your point, I'll state mine. Until one of us capitulates.'

'I've wanted you from the first moment I saw you.'

He'd lowered his voice and it was throaty, the sound that echoed through her whole body.

'Is that your first point?'

'Oh, yes.'

'Mine is that wanting a woman is not a sufficient criterion for having her. You'll have to come up with a better argument, Mr MacAllister.'

'How about this: you've wanted me from the first moment you saw me, too.'

'I object. That is speculation.'

Angus shook his head, smiling. 'I beg to differ. It's not speculation. One of the first things you said to me was, 'Mr MacAllister, perhaps you should fetch your chicken.' I've never heard a more blatant invitation.'

She pressed her lips tight together to keep from laughing. 'Is that your point?'

'No. This is my point.' He moved the inch over that she'd scootched away, so his thigh rested against hers again, and put his arm around her shoulders.

'Excuse me, Mr MacAllister. This is an intellectual sport, not a physical one.'

'They taught us how to debate dirty at my school.' He pulled her still closer to him. 'Besides, with us, it's an attraction of bodies and minds.'

'Well. Two can play at that game.' She swivelled in her seat and draped her legs over Angus's lap. Marvelling at how much she was enjoying this, at how she and Angus were able to make their own private intimate space even when there were others around, even now, when they were surrounded by the lights and the people and the traffic of London outside the cab's windows.

'Is that your point?' In the shifting light from the streets, she could see his eyes twinkle.

'No. That's me doing my best to distract you so that you won't be able to think up an effective rebuttal to the point I do make.'

'Good tactic.' He put his free hand on her knee and stroked up her leg to where her dress had ridden up. 'You're driving me crazy, Miss Read. I move that we change the topic of this debate to "This house believes that when you and I make love it will be the most amazing experience in the universe".'

'Denied. You still haven't won the first debate yet.'

'Haven't I?' He slid his hand further up her leg, underneath the hem of her dress. His thumb brushed the top of her thigh, tantalisingly close to her knickers.

Elisabeth didn't know what would be sexier—toying with Angus some more, or giving in to his caresses.

Since they were still in a taxi, though, it was probably wiser to refrain from tearing off her clothes for now.

'I still haven't made my point,' she said.

Angus leaned forward, his hand touching the lace of her underwear now, his lips a breath away from hers. 'And your point is?'

She'd forgotten. But she was damned if she was going to admit it.

'My point is that you're a bounder, a cad, an incorrigible flirt and a sensualist with whom a lady cannot be safe.'

'I object. I am not a bounder.' His voice was even more English and upper-class than normal. 'I have a suspicion you like it when I'm a cad, though.'

He feathered his fingertips over the lace covering her sex, and Elisabeth gasped.

The cab stopped.

In an instant Angus had withdrawn from her, given the driver a note through the window and was opening the door and holding out a hand to help her out of the cab. She took it, feeling slightly dizzy and very aroused.

It wasn't a cold night, but her heated skin felt the change in temperature. Traffic noises, flashing lights, plane trees and a row of tall white Georgian town houses.

'Where are we?' she asked.

'Notting Hill. Outside my house. Who won the debate?'

She thought back to their conversation and added it up. 'You made one point which was spurious, with one discounted because it was speculation. And lots of cheating. Whereas I only cheated once, and made two valid points. I've won.'

'You might have won the intellectual debate. I won the physical one. I gained an arm around your shoulder, and a hand on your leg.'

'We didn't agree to a physical debate.'

Angus half inclined his head. 'All right. I capitulate. The question is, since you won: are you coming in, or am I calling you another cab?'

# CHAPTER SEVEN

ELISABETH hesitated for a split second, and Angus couldn't breathe. Then she smiled, that heart-lifting, spirited, kind smile.

'I'm coming in,' she said. And once again Angus felt overwhelming relief.

'What made you decide?' he asked, squeezing her hand. 'Was it my superior debating skills?'

'No. It was when you said that we would play.' She felt the lapel of his jacket, smoothed down his shirt. Simple touches that turned him on enormously. Her brown eyes as they met his glimmered deep and dark in the light from the streetlamps.

'I need to have fun, Angus. I need some romance and some fantasy. I haven't had anything like that for too long.'

'Elisabeth, I knew that as soon as I saw you order filter coffee with skim milk in the best Italian café in London.'

He bent down, slid one arm around her waist, one around her legs, and swept Elisabeth up into his arms. 'Fun, fantasy, and romance coming right up.'

She felt wonderful in his arms—graceful and slender and yielding and as if she belonged there. He could see the length of each of her legs, feel how her flexible waist fit his hand.

He took the steps up to his house two at a time. He'd take the steps up to his bedroom three at a time, if he could.

And then, at his black glossy front door, he had to stop. 'Um,' he said.

'What's wrong, MacAllister?'

'I think this romantic gesture was a little ill-planned. Do you mind reaching into my left trouser pocket and getting out my keys? My hands are sort of full.'

Elisabeth laughed and reached downwards. He closed his eyes and gritted his teeth as her hand felt around the front of his trousers searching for his pocket. Her palm brushed over the head of his penis. He'd had an erection for hours, it seemed. And her hand was sweet heaven.

'Angus.' Elisabeth's voice was full of mock horror, and he knew she hadn't been fumbling.

He groaned. 'Get the keys or I'll be happy to see you naked on this doorstep.'

Her fingers, now, were swift and sure. She pulled his keys out of his pocket and with his instructions fitted them into the locks. As soon as she turned the last one he kicked the door open. It swung open with a satisfying bang. He carried Elisabeth over the threshold, hooked the door with his foot, and slammed it shut behind them.

Angus stood in the black-and-white tiled hallway of his house with Elisabeth in his arms and let out a huge sigh. 'Thank God.'

'What?' A hint of a smile was playing over her beautiful mouth.

'Finally I've got you alone in a place that isn't a classroom or a refrigerator, and I can take all the time that I want.'

'Do you want to take a long time?'

'Oh-h-h, yes. And I intend to savour every moment.' He strode across the hall to the staircase. 'Forgive my being a bad host, but I'm not going to ask you if you'd like a drink because I want you in my bedroom. Is being carried up the steps Scarlett O'Hara-style romantic enough for you?'

'Angus.'

Her speaking his name made him pause, his foot raised to take the first stair. He looked at her.

That little smile was gone. And her pale, classical face looked even paler than usual, her eyes huge.

He frowned. 'What is it, Elisabeth?'

'I—' She bit her lip. She was lost for words.

Anxiety crawled into his stomach. If she was having second thoughts…if she didn't trust him…

'What, darling? You can tell me.'

He saw her graceful throat swallow. 'Do—do you have condoms? I don't—' Her pale cheeks flushed peony.

'Oh.' He laughed in relief. She was worried about safe sex, nothing more. Prudent, sensible, adorable teacher. 'Yes. Yes, I've got some of those.' He raised his foot again to climb the steps.

'Good.'

And yet the way she said it made him put his foot back down on the floor.

Something wasn't good at all.

'What's wrong?'

'I—' She dropped her eyes, and then a line of determination appeared between her brows and she looked up straight into his face. 'I haven't had sex for fun for a long time. I'm not sure I remember how.'

She was honest, and open, and brave. She didn't have to admit this to him, and he knew it. Angus tightened his arms around her.

'Elisabeth,' he said, 'all you have to do tonight is to feel pleasure. I want to make you feel wonderful. Will you let me do that?'

She nodded. English teacher still with no words.

'I mean it,' he said. 'No pretending tonight, unless it's in fun. All I want is to have you with me, to touch you, to show you how much I want you. You don't have to be afraid or put up any of your defences.'

'Help me do that,' she said. 'I need to.'

And this was trust beyond what he'd dreamed of, a challenge and a reward. He wasn't just going to give her what she wanted; he was going to give her what she needed.

He kissed her coral lips, and again.

'I think this is going to be one of the best nights of my life,' he said to her, and started climbing the stairs at last.

His bedroom was large and modern. Tall windows looked out onto a dark blue and orange London night and threw panes of light and shadow across the carpet. The sheets on his bed were white.

He stepped inside the door with her in his arms and carried her to the side of his bed, where he set her on her feet on the floor.

He closed the blinds, then reached down and turned on the lamp on the bedside table. It wasn't bright, but it bathed the room in a golden glow that was more revealing than the evening shadows.

And this man dated the most beautiful women in the country. He was in the tabloids with them every weekend.

Elisabeth didn't mind her body. Though it didn't always do what she wanted it to, it was more or less the shape she wanted it to be in. But she was no model.

'Do we have to have the light on?' she asked.

Angus nodded vehemently. 'I want to touch and smell and taste and hear you. I want to see you, too.'

He reached forward and pulled out the pins that held up her hair, and she felt it falling around her face, down the bare back of her neck. He ran his hands through it, smoothing the straight locks back into place.

The look of concentration and appreciation on his face quieted her doubts. He stepped back and once again looked her over, up and down, taking in every inch with his eyes.

Her lipstick was kissed away, her dress was wrinkled, and she could see that Angus did not care. She could see that Angus found her even more appealing because of it. He slowly ran one hand across the neckline of her dress, touching the green glass necklace. 'This is pretty on you. You always have something exotic.'

'It's my zen necklace,' she told him. 'Be here now.'

'Good advice. Turn around.'

She turned and felt his deft hands holding up her hair, unfastening her necklace and lifting it from her throat. His soft breaths were on the back of her neck. And then his lips at the place where the clasp had been, warm and gentle and shivering her skin into goose-flesh.

'Have I found an erogenous zone, Miss Read?' he murmured and kissed a trail along her nape and to the skin beneath her ear. Every one sizzled through her.

'Yes.' Though she didn't have to say it; he could surely see the small hairs of her arm and her nape standing to attention.

'Hmm. I wonder where the other ones are.' He tugged at the zip at the back of her dress and drew it down to where it ended, just above the curve of her buttocks. His knuckles brushed the small of her back and she shuddered.

'Found one,' he said, and she could tell from the sound of his voice that he was smiling. Then he kissed down her neck, between her shoulder blades, down her spine. She held her breath and felt his warm hands slip inside her dress, span her waist. His finger-tips rested on her belly; his thumbs framed the small of her back. Slowly he touched his lips to her skin there, just above her tailbone.

She felt it to the tips of her fingers and the ends of her toes.

With Angus behind her, she couldn't see him. But she could picture his beautiful hands around her waist, his incredible mouth as it kissed her, drew slow circles with his tongue.

And he wasn't even at the main erogenous zones yet. And she was still nearly dressed.

'Angus,' she choked, and gripped the headboard of his bed to stop from tumbling forward.

'I bet you anything you're ticklish,' he said against her back, and she felt the vibration of his voice and gripped the bed even tighter.

'Don't,' she warned.

His hands moved lazily up and down her waist. 'Did you know,' he said between kisses, exploring either side of her spine, 'that laughing is very close to having an orgasm?'

'You wouldn't dare.'

Instead of the tickling onslaught she expected, he made his way back up her spine to her neck and whispered in her ear. 'I'm the type of man who takes dares.'

Before she could register what he was doing he slipped her dress off her shoulders. It slithered down her body and landed in a pool at her feet until she was standing in her black underwear and high heels.

'Oh, God, Elisabeth,' he muttered, his raspy voice even deeper. His hands settled on her waist again and this time when she looked down she could see them, big and long-fingered and scarred.

Gently he turned her around, and for a moment he just stood there, his hands on her waist, looking at her. Her heart was beating so hard that she thought he could probably see it hammering against her ribcage.

'You are stunning,' he said.

'I'd like the chance to return the compliment, but you still have all of your clothes on,' Elisabeth replied.

He nodded. 'And that's the way I'm going to keep it for a little while. I don't want to be tempted to rush. Sit down, sweetheart.'

Angus MacAllister calling all the shots, fully dressed while she was in her underwear. As if he knew that she needed to lose control, and was therefore subtly taking it from her.

She thought about all the pleasure he said he wanted to give to her. How much she wanted to be in his hands.

Elisabeth sat down on the bed and Angus knelt in front of her. He took one of her feet on his knee and cradled her calf in one of his hands while he unstrapped her shoe with the other. 'I hope you never wear these shoes to school,' he said, pulling it off and dropping a kiss on the top of her foot.

'Are you joking? I'd break my neck while I was chasing after smokers on the playground.'

He took her other foot. 'I meant that you'd probably give your male students and colleagues heart attacks.' He removed her second shoe, and ran a light-feather fingertip up the bottom of her foot.

She shuddered. Even that small touch was intense.

'Another erogenous zone?'

'Evidently,' she said shakily. 'You're not really going to tickle me, are you?'

'Ah.' His eyes were mischievous. 'Anticipation and uncertainty are half the pleasure.'

'I'm not so sure about that.'

'It's true. Think about trying out a new recipe, a new restaurant. You think it's going to be good—you like the ingredients, you've read good reviews—but it's new. Could be a disaster. The recipe could have salt instead of sugar or the chef could be off with pneumonia.'

As he spoke he slowly, slowly let his hands creep up the inside of her legs, from calf to knee to thigh. Inch by inch.

'But from the first moment you decide to try something new,

you start to look forward to it.' Another inch up her thigh. He was halfway up, and then more than halfway up.

'You start being desperate for it.'

She watched his hands. The way the bones of the backs of them moved, so precise and strong, with every caress. Up another inch. Just half an inch, now, from the material of her knickers. She glanced at his face, which was still, intent, focused on the small space of skin between his hands and her crotch.

He'd touch her. Any moment. She felt swollen, yearning, desperate. She held her breath.

'You start,' he murmured, 'thinking you can't wait another second.'

She pictured watching his fingers pushing her underwear aside, caressing her gently, with the wonderful magic he could create. Slipping inside her.

'Please,' she breathed.

He'd leaned forward; she could feel his breath on the bare skin of her belly. He closed the small distance between them and kissed her below her belly button. His hands moved no closer to where she was more than desperate for him now, she was on the brink of insanity, she was ready to grab his hand and put it on her and as soon as she did she would climax, she knew it.

His hands moved.

Up from her thighs, to her waist and ribs, where they rippled and tickled.

Elisabeth shrieked.

She fell back on the bed, trying to wriggle away from him, but he laughed and climbed on top of her, his legs pinning hers down. His hands danced over her stomach, her sides, and Elisabeth laughed and gasped for breath.

'Was I right?' he asked. 'Was it half the pleasure?'

'No!' she cried, and then he tickled more. 'Yes!'

'Which is it?' He redoubled his efforts and Elisabeth giggled, tears squeezing from her eyes. 'No, or yes?'

'Yes!'

'Don't forget the "Chef".'

'Yes, Chef! Let me breathe!'

Angus stopped tickling her and collapsed beside her on the bed. Elisabeth wiped the tears from her eyes. His hair and suit were rumpled; his cheeks were flushed, and his eyes sparkled.

He wasn't just sexy. He was funny, and playful, and intelligent, and, in a strange way, vulnerable.

'I love to hear you laugh,' he said. He reached over and took her in his arms and kissed her.

And her ticklish spots were erogenous too, because with the touch of his lips to hers she was twice as desperate as before. She dug her fingers into his shoulders and wound her leg around his. The material of his suit was soft against her belly, her inner thigh, his shirt crisp against her chest, and she could feel his erection against her again. She arched against him and pushed his jacket from his shoulders.

Angus shrugged it off and moved so that he was lying on top of her, the length of his body against her. The hard ridge of his arousal pressed between her legs.

Elisabeth strained herself upwards, pushed up her hips into him, wanting to increase the pressure, find release. She kissed him savagely, biting at his bottom lip, answering the sexual thrusts of his tongue with her own. She made pleading sounds in the back of her throat and when he pulled his lips away from hers to kiss his leisurely way down her neck and chest she panted, every breath full of his scent.

'Please, Angus,' she said. She heard him chuckle and felt his soft hair brush the side of her neck as he shook his head.

'I've waited far too long for you,' he said. 'I'm going to take all the time I like.'

'Well, I've been waiting just as long and I say touch me now, please.' She pushed her hips upwards again just in case he didn't know what she was talking about.

He propped himself up on his elbows above her. 'I'm setting the pace, here, remember? You said you'd let me give you pleasure.'

'Uh-huh. And if you don't hurry up and give it to me I think I'm going to go out of my mind.'

'That's exactly what I've got planned,' he said, and reached down and unfastened her bra. Elisabeth moaned as he took her breasts into his scarred, talented hands. And then, even more incredible, he dipped his head and caught one of her nipples in his hot, wet mouth.

She cried out and twined her fingers in his hair to hold him to her breast as he tasted her. He pressed kisses to her flesh, and then sucked her nipple deep. And then slowly made his way to her other breast and did the same exquisite thing.

'You are beautiful,' he murmured against her. His words made little cool puffs of air against her wet nipple, swollen from his attentions. He touched it lightly with his tongue and then held it between his lips, nipping with gentle care with his teeth.

She could no longer see straight. Elisabeth reached down and grabbed his right hand and brought it between her legs. 'Now,' she said.

He chuckled, a very male sound of amusement and arousal. 'You're used to having your orders obeyed, aren't you?'

'As long as you obey this one, I'll be very happy.'

Angus raised himself to his knees and curled his fingers around the waistband of her knickers. 'The pleasure will be mutual,' he said, and carefully slid her underwear down her legs.

He knelt there between her legs, looking at her. She saw him swallow and bite his lip.

Then he touched her.

A single, long stroke at first. And another. Skilful, delicate, reverent touches.

She threw her head back, abandoning herself to the pleasure his hands gave her. All of her nerve endings felt concentrated on that one small nub of flesh where his fingers caressed and circled.

She felt all the desire, all the tension, all the emotion she had tried so hard to contain for so long, rising in her towards release. She lifted her hips towards him.

Angus stilled his hand.

'Give me another order,' he whispered.

'Don't stop.'

'Like this?'

He moved his hand infinitely slowly. Elisabeth felt sweat

breaking out at every pore of her body. She raised her head and looked at Angus.

His concentration on her was complete, a sexy half-smile on his face. His eyes followed his hand as he feathered his fingertips over her. She could feel his attention, his gaze like another touch.

Then he slid a single finger of his left hand into her.

Elisabeth screamed, grabbed the blankets, closed her eyes as her orgasm pounded through her. First in great wrenching waves, making her thrash her body on the bed. Then gentler, still thrilling, like little electric shocks.

Angus kept on touching her, even as her contractions subsided, even as she gasped for breath. He didn't stop. He kept up his steady, skilled caresses, as if he wanted to bring her to a point beyond orgasm, to an ecstasy that she'd never dreamed before.

She'd closed her eyes; she opened them. He was still rapt, his face focused on her.

His touch became too exquisite. Elisabeth felt ticklish—not only between her legs, but everywhere, her whole skin tingling and giggling.

She burst into laughter and tried to wriggle away from him. 'Stop—Angus, it tickles.'

'Laughter is close to orgasm. And orgasm is close to laughter.' He looked up, his eyes sparkling. 'I think my two favourite sounds are you doing both.'

Even before her giggles had melted away he had shifted suddenly on the bed and replaced his hands with his mouth.

Elisabeth cried out in surprise and pleasure. His mouth felt different from his hands, wet and hot and clever, and what had been ticklish became achingly arousing.

Last time had been slow. This time was fast. His lips and teeth and tongue built the passion to a peak so quickly she barely understood the stages until she was shaking in the grip of another, even more intense orgasm.

He held onto her hips, tight, as she rode it through to the aftershocks, and then he moved up the bed to gather her to him. She clung on to him through his clothes and tried to catch her breath.

'You're wonderful,' he whispered to her, and kissed her. She could taste herself on his lips.

'I'm—oh, my God, Angus, that was unbelievable.'

'Yes, it was.' He kissed her on her forehead, gentle and soft, stroked back her damp hair with one hand, and Elisabeth closed her eyes to savour this feeling. Naked with Angus, his body cradling hers. His heartbeat strong against her breast.

'Thank you,' she said, curling closer to him. Contentment spread its languid way through her veins. She lifted her face without opening her eyes and kissed him. 'I've never felt anything like that.'

She could feel him smiling even without looking. 'And we're not even finished yet,' he said.

'I know.' She reached over and twined her fingers through his and put her other palm on his chest and felt his breathing. She hadn't felt so relaxed for such a long time. After all her worrying, all her fighting herself and fighting him. She was home.

'I want to see you naked,' she murmured. 'I want you inside me. And I want...'

She fell asleep.

# CHAPTER EIGHT

*Too bright and too hot.*

Angus opened one of his eyes and immediately shut it again. A ray of sunlight pierced through a gap in the blinds and shone directly into his eye.

It was morning. Careful not to disturb Elisabeth, who lay graceful and precious against him, he shifted his head to one side on the pillow, away from the sunbeam.

She hadn't moved since last night. The same slight smile was on her face. Her dark eyelashes rested on her cheeks, just flushed with sleep. The swell of her breasts was hidden against his chest; one of her bare long legs was draped over his leg, still in his wrinkled trousers.

She was the most beautiful sight he'd ever seen. Angus smiled, remembering how she'd fallen asleep while demanding sex from him. Mid-sentence. He'd shaken her gently, whispered her name. No luck. She'd been out.

Some men might take that as an insult, he supposed.

He'd shrugged and taken it as a compliment. She lay in his arms, as trusting as when she'd lain naked beneath him and abandoned herself to his touch.

He'd breathed in her scent and tightened his arms around her, and closed his eyes. Fallen asleep himself.

And now it was—Angus glanced at his bedside clock. And blinked and checked it again.

*Half past nine?*

He couldn't remember having slept this late in years. And it hadn't been very late in the evening when they'd fallen asleep, either. On a conservative estimate, they'd just slept for ten hours. Without moving once.

Angus shook his head. He'd trained himself to get by on six hours' sleep at a time, at most. During his working hours he practically had pure espresso running through his veins.

Well. Apparently Elisabeth had needed the sleep, and he had too.

Elisabeth stirred, and stretched herself against him like a lazy cat. The movement arched her belly against him, curved her spine back so he could see the rosy tips of her breasts.

Angus felt something a lot stronger than caffeine in his blood. The sleep wasn't all he needed.

He put his hand on the curve of her hip, pulled her more snugly against what was rapidly turning into a raging erection, and sighed in pleasure.

Elisabeth opened her eyes. They were brown and clear and gorgeous.

'Hi,' she said, her voice still husky with sleep. Then her eyes widened, and she pushed herself up on one elbow.

'Oh, my God. Did I fall asleep right in the middle of everything?'

He nodded, and she blushed bright pink.

'I am so, so sorry, Angus. I don't know why— It wasn't—I must have been tired—'

And he loved it when she couldn't get the words right. He kissed her lips. 'It's fine,' he said. 'I was tired too. And I enjoyed sleeping with you.'

Her mouth twitched with humour. 'Is that the literal sleeping with me, or the euphemistic sleeping with me?'

'Both. Though we haven't really completed the euphemism yet.'

Her smile grew. 'I'm so relieved to hear you say that. I would've hated to have missed out on anything while I was asleep.' Her hands went to his shirt, started unbuttoning.

He feigned outrage. 'Elisabeth, believe me, if we'd been doing the euphemism, you'd have been wide awake and shouting my name to the rooftops.'

'You are so arrogant.' She pushed his shirt from his shoulders and laid a warm kiss on his chest. Her hair brushed his bare skin.

'Check your dictionary, teacher. It's not arrogance if it's the truth.'

Her palms ran up and down his ribcage. 'I think you should check your own dictionary, Chef. Because last time I looked the entry for "super stud" didn't have the words "falls asleep in his clothes" in it.'

'Blasted English teachers,' he muttered roughly. Her teasing talk was building his desire as much as her curious hands. 'If you have some marking or lesson planning to do, I could drive you home right now.'

Her fingers paused at the button of his trousers. 'Do you really want me to call your bluff on that one, Angus?'

'No. No, I don't.'

She smiled. 'Good.' With deft fingers she unfastened his trousers and pushed them down over his hips. Angus reached down and helped her, taking off his boxer shorts and kicking off his socks while he was at it.

Naked with Elisabeth. At last. He reached for her.

She beat him to it, putting her palms on his shoulders and pushing him over onto his back. She straddled his legs.

He took her in, her elegant collar-bone and shoulders, her beautiful breasts, her softly curved stomach and hips. He'd looked his fill last night, but he still wanted more.

He saw the contrast between her pale feminine body and his harder planes; the soft strength of her thighs and his jutting arousal. She was looking at him, too; her eyes were wide and full of passion. He groaned and raised his hands to touch her breasts, to pull her down and taste her.

The phone rang.

Of course, he had an extension by his bed. Just in the unlikely case that he happened to be sleeping when somebody needed him.

It rang again. His restaurant, his publisher, the BBC, any one of dozens of people to whom he owed his success and his fame.

With one hand, he held Elisabeth in place on top of him while he twisted his torso to the left. With the other, he reached over the side of the bed to the telephone.

By feel, he found the cord connecting the phone to the socket. And ripped it out of the wall.

'Sorry about that.' He smiled up at her, settling onto his back again. 'Where were we?'

'About here, I think.' She put her hand down and wrapped her fingers around his erection.

Oh, good Lord.

Angus had spent a great deal of his adult life in search of physical pleasure. The most exquisite smells, the most satisfying textures and tastes. The full-body rush of adrenaline that came from working hard and succeeding.

This simple touch, five fingers of a delicate hand on his skin, surpassed them all.

She caressed up his length, and he wouldn't've thought it possible but he felt himself growing still harder. She bent down to him and he seized the back of her head, pulled her to him and kissed her more hungrily than he'd ever kissed any woman. Relishing the sensation of her breasts on his chest, her legs around him.

'Where's the condom?' she gasped when they parted.

He reached to the side again, this time to open the bedside drawer and feel out a packet. She took it from his hand, opened it, and stroked the condom onto him.

He watched her face as she positioned herself over him and guided him into her, inch by exciting inch. Her mouth was open, wet from his kiss, curled in half a wondering smile; her eyelids fluttered in pleasure.

She felt it as intensely as he did, how perfectly their bodies fit together. She was tight and hot around him. Quite simply the most thrilling sensation he had ever experienced.

Except when she began to move on him, and it got even better.

'Oh, Elisabeth, oh, darling,' he muttered as he let his hands explore her. Her hands still rested on his shoulders, holding him down, holding her up. She set the pace for their movements, leisurely enough to feel every nuance of pleasure, quick enough to show how desperate she was for him, too, and Angus realised with a smile that Elisabeth was taking back the control she had abandoned to him the night before.

And the heat was building, her movements becoming by small degrees wilder. He dug his heels into the bed and met her, thrust for thrust, so deep inside her he felt as if he were part of her.

He remembered her orgasm the night before, how powerfully she had contracted around his hand, how her face had looked when she came. He slipped a hand between their bodies and found her clitoris, and gasped with her when he felt her jolt of pleasure with his own body.

Two more thrusts, a small flicker of his thumb, and her hands fisted on his shoulders. She threw back her head and let out a wordless cry as he felt her shudder around him.

And even better. With her body enveloping him, moving to the rhythm of his own blood, her scent in his nostrils, cinnamon and sweet woman, her taste on his lips, his hands full of Elisabeth, he felt his climax rip through his body.

'Elisabeth!' he yelled, and raised his hips from the bed to thrust deep, one last amazing time. Every fibre of him. With her.

She collapsed forward onto him and he wrapped his arms around her. Held her so close he couldn't tell whose heartbeat he felt.

And then realised that she was giggling.

'What?' He pushed her hair back from her face so he could see her smile.

'You shouted my name to the rooftops,' she said.

He laughed. 'You always win, don't you?' He kissed her, and again. 'I think you're fantastic.'

'Funny, I was going to say the same thing about you.'

She wiggled off him so she was lying beside him and he watched her, fascinated by the movement of her hips, torso, breasts. She propped herself up on her elbow and he could see that she, too, was looking at his body, desire still in her eyes.

'I think you broke your phone,' she said.

'Not important,' he said. 'Elisabeth, I love looking at you naked.'

She nodded. 'You're the most beautiful man I've ever seen. I think I might make you get up and walk around for me in a minute so I can appreciate you.'

'In a minute.' He captured her mouth in another kiss.

Her stomach growled loudly.

Elisabeth giggled again, and put her hand on her stomach. 'Oops. Guess I'm hungry for food, too.'

'Good. I'll make us breakfast.' He planted a last kiss on her cheek, a final caress of her arm, before he stood up and disposed of the condom. Elisabeth lay there in bed watching him. She looked rumpled, satisfied, breathtaking, her dark hair spread on his pillow, her tall body relaxed.

He took his time walking to the closet to get some clothes, enjoying her eyes on him. When he got there he glanced back over his shoulder at her. Snagged a robe and a pair of jeans, did a catwalk turn, and went back to the bedside.

She was grinning. 'Modest, aren't you?'

He shrugged. 'Hey, if you've got it, you might as well use it. I was voted fifth best Rear of the Year by *Celeb Monthly* magazine.'

'You should have won.'

'I would have, if they'd allowed me to take my chef whites off in the photo shoot.' He winked at her and pulled on his jeans.

'You're incorrigible.'

'And that's exactly what you like about me.' He nodded towards the robe he'd laid on the bed beside her. 'I'll go and put on the coffee and get some eggs. If you get the shower hot I might join you before I start cooking.'

Angus hummed to himself as he went down the stairs, walked past the phone with its blinking answering machine in his living room, and ground the beans for coffee in his kitchen. The sun was gleaming off every surface of his kitchen, the coffee smelled rich and wonderful, and Angus felt great. Whistling, he unlocked the door to the back garden and stepped into the sunshine.

Even so early in the day, the sun had warmed his herb garden and the aroma rose to meet him as he passed. His two chickens stopped scratching around and came to the end of their run when he approached.

'Morning MacNugget, Kiev,' he greeted them and replenished their food and water while they clucked quietly, their feathers bright. While they were busy eating he slipped into their coop and found two still-warm eggs.

Brilliant. This was turning out to be the perfect day all round, he thought as he cut a bunch of fragrant herbs in the garden. He would put out two mugs ready for coffee, lose the jeans, and go upstairs to join Elisabeth in the shower.

He was so pleased with his plan that he didn't spot the tall blonde woman standing in his kitchen drinking his coffee until he was already inside.

'Where have you been?' she demanded, putting down her cup.

'Good morning, Christine.' He set down the eggs and smiled at his publicist. 'Do help yourself to coffee.'

'I've been ringing you all morning and haven't been able to get through.'

'That's because I haven't been answering my phone,' he said pleasantly, feeling his shower plans slipping down the drain. 'How'd you get in?'

'You gave me a key for that photo shoot in March, remember? I called Magnum and they hadn't seen you either. I thought you might be sick.'

'I've never been better in my life.' He leaned back against the counter and folded his arms across his bare chest. 'How are you?'

'I'm going mad. I've got the tabloids ringing me every five minutes trying to confirm these interviews with you, I've got a press pack ready to go out waiting for your approval, I've got a conference call with Los Angeles this afternoon to talk about syndication for your show, and you've gone all anti-communication all of a sudden.'

Angus watched Christine pour herself more coffee and add non-calorie sweetener from her handbag. 'Don't any of these people ever take the weekend off?' he asked.

'Well, we could have sorted this all out last night if you'd only talked with me. Listen.' She sat down at his kitchen table.

Angus was listening; he could hear the water running in the upstairs shower. Elisabeth was underneath the spray now, warm drops running down her naked body. He wondered what water would taste like sipped from her skin.

'So I've scheduled you in with the *Herald* on Monday and the *Journal* on Tuesday. But I'm not happy about the deal you agreed with the Slater School. They're still saying no cameras, not even a five-minute tie-in for your show. You can talk about the contest in the press but you can't go into detail about the kids. As it stands now, this is a publicity gambit with hardly any publicity attached to it, aside from filming the competition at the end. I've been trying to negotiate with the head teacher for the past month and he won't budge. I'm sorry, Angus, but it's a waste of your time and mine. You really might as well give it up.'

'I'm not giving it up.'

Christine glanced at him sharply, surprised by something in his tone.

'Fine,' she said. 'It's your time to waste. But if you're determined not to quit, we might as well make something out of it. I suggest we arrange a tip-off to the press about the kids. Something subtle. They can find the rest out themselves. That way we'll get better coverage, you can be forced to say something selfless about helping young people, and we can claim we had nothing to do with it.'

Angus thought about what a media spotlight would do to Jennifer's fledgling confidence. How Danny, who didn't know how to react to attention, would deal with being in the news.

He thought about the trust that Elisabeth had started to give him.

'No,' he said.

Christine's expression was even more surprised. 'Okay, you don't want to go back on an agreement, fair enough. We'll just do the interviews, and maybe the press will be bright enough to work it out. It wouldn't be the first time.'

'No. No interviews at all. I'm not talking to the press until this competition is over. I don't want the competition to be filmed, either. In fact I want to keep as low a profile as possible.'

Christine frowned. 'Angus, what's going on with you? When you hired me, you said you wanted to be the best-known chef of your generation. You said you'd do anything as long as it didn't get in the way of your cooking.'

'Well, my priorities have changed.' He opened a cupboard and got out an omelette pan. 'It's great seeing you, Christine, but I've got a guest for breakfast, so—'

'Where were you? I was looking forward to soaping—oh.'

The startled voice came from the doorway, where Elisabeth

stood wrapped in his robe, her hair wet and her cheeks flushed. 'I'm sorry, I thought—'

'Elisabeth.' Angus went to her and put his arm around her shoulders. 'Darling, this is Christine Butler, my publicist, who dropped in for a moment. Christine, this is Elisabeth Read.'

'Your breakfast guest.' Christine stood and shook hands with Elisabeth. 'It's so lovely to meet you, Elisabeth, and I'm very sorry to interrupt. You must excuse me, I have a phone call or two to make, but I do hope to see you again.'

'I'll see you out,' Angus said, and squeezed Elisabeth's shoulders before following Christine out of the kitchen and through his living room to the front door.

'I understand your change of priorities,' Christine said to him in a low tone, her eyebrows raised in amusement. 'That's the teacher, isn't it?'

'I don't want the press involved.'

She shrugged her narrow shoulders. 'Fair enough. Though she's going to have to deal with it sooner or later if she's going to stick around.'

'And that's for her to decide. Not the media.'

Christine smiled and pecked him on the cheek. 'She looks charming. Give me a ring if your priorities change again.'

'Go home and relax, Christine. Enjoy the weekend.'

'I don't need to tell you to enjoy it yourself.' She went down his front stairs, her car keys jingling.

When Angus got back to the kitchen, Elisabeth was standing exactly where he'd left her. 'Sorry about that,' he said. 'I wasn't expecting Christine today.'

'That's fine. Of course you have a life and a career,' Elisabeth said, but he could see some of the tightness returning to her face again.

'Hey.' He took her in his arms and held her until he felt her relax a little. She smelled of his shampoo. It smelled better on her. 'I'm sorry your shower was lonely.' He let his hands creep inside the robe and rest on her bare waist.

She shrugged. 'Just as well. If you'd joined me we'd still be in there and I'm hungry.'

'How about this,' he said. 'We'll have coffee, I'll make break-fast, we'll bring it up to bed and then we'll take another shower together. And then I'll make some phone calls and cancel my appointments until Monday.' He was meant to be at Magnum this weekend, but Henry and the team could handle it without him.

'I deserve a weekend off,' he said. 'And I want to spend it with you.'

Elisabeth smiled and settled closer into his embrace. 'I deserve a weekend off too. Listen, I'm sorry I drove your publicist away if you had to talk business.'

He was tempted to explain the conversation he'd just had with Christine, but then he thought better of it. He'd only recently convinced Elisabeth that he was interested in Jennifer and Danny's welfare in the first place. It wouldn't do any good to remind her that this whole thing had started out as a publicity scheme.

Especially since the publicity angle wasn't even going to happen.

He kissed her, and said, 'It wasn't important.'

Although he thought maybe it was the most important decision he'd made in a long time.

# CHAPTER NINE

THE interior of Luciano's looked the same: dark walls, marble-topped tables, the grey-haired Italian man behind the counter near the espresso machine. Angus MacAllister looked the same: tall, smiling, dimple-chinned, tempting.

Elisabeth supposed she probably looked the same, too, except for the odd collection of clothes she was wearing—her little black dress with a designer shirt of Angus's knotted over the top, and a pair of flat beaded shoes she'd picked up the day before browsing in the Portobello Road Saturday market.

Aside from the clothes and the day of the week it was all exactly the same as the last time they'd been here together, Elisabeth thought. The only things that had changed weren't visible.

She slid into her seat laughing, shaking off the sparse rain-drops from her hair, as Angus shouted a greeting to Luciano in Italian. They'd seen the rain clouds approaching as they'd walked hand in hand through Kensington Gardens and Angus had bet her a coffee that they'd make it to Luciano's before it started raining.

Angus's Italian was considerably better than hers, but when she recognised the words *'caffè filtrato'* she put her hand on his arm to stop him ordering her filter coffee with skimmed milk.

'I'll have a cappuccino this time,' she said.

Angus's smile was blinding. He kissed her on the cheek. 'You won't regret it.'

'Best in London, I hear.'

The rest of his order was incomprehensible to her, so she had no idea what Angus and Luciano were laughing about as Angus pulled his chair over to be closer to her and sat down.

'Everybody in the world likes you,' she marvelled.

'Why wouldn't they? I'm a nice bloke.'

'Yes, but I mean everybody. Every single person we've spoken to this weekend was happy to see you—all the stallholders in Portobello Road, the publican at lunch today. Even strangers say hello to you.'

He shrugged. 'It's the nice side of being famous.'

She shook her head. 'No, it's not that. You work hard for it. I'll never forget how you charmed Harjeet at school in under five minutes. And what you've done with Jennifer and Danny. It's important to you that people like you, isn't it?'

Luciano came with their coffees and a plate of flaky almond-crusted pastries and exchanged another joke with Angus in Italian before he went back behind his counter. Angus picked up his espresso, took a sip with his eyes closed in appreciation, and then put his cup down contemplatively.

'It's always been important,' he said. 'It started out as a coping strategy, I suppose. My parents never wanted to have very much to do with me. They were so spectacularly uninterested in who I was that I saw them exactly four times between the ages of twelve and sixteen.' He took another sip of his coffee. 'I guess I've always wanted to prove that I was likeable.'

She touched the back of his hand, running her finger along one of the jagged scars. 'Where did you go during the school holidays?'

'To friends' houses, mainly. Or to our house in the Scottish Highlands; we had staff there. Once I got there and they'd given the staff a holiday—forgot I was coming home, I think. I was ten years old and I spent the entire Easter holiday alone.' His face was wry, but Elisabeth could see the hurt. 'That's when I first discovered how to cook.'

'Where are they now?'

'Abroad somewhere—that's what they do. They have a house in London, but I haven't been there since I was sixteen and I announced to my tutor that I was going to quit school and apprentice in a kitchen. My parents were so appalled that they flew over from Buenos Aires and shut me in the house in Belgravia for a week trying to talk me out of it. Eventually I climbed out the window.' He laughed. 'I'm more like Danny than you think I am.'

'I'm sorry, Angus.'

She pictured Angus as a boy, dark-haired and slender, wandering the venerable corridors of his school, laughing, joking, making as many friends as he could to fill up his loneliness.

Her own childhood had had plenty of lonely times. But she'd never actually been alone. And, she realised now, she'd always been safe—even if she hadn't felt it at the time.

'My parents were a little strange,' she said, 'but they were always there. They loved me. Even if they did spend most of the eighties living in nudist camps.'

Angus laughed. 'If I'd had the choice of parents, I'd have chosen nude Canadian hippies.'

'You would've got bored with the lentils, though.' She took a sip of her cappuccino. It was frothy, creamy, and divine. 'You're right about the coffee.'

He nodded absently. 'You say everybody likes me. But you didn't like me when you first met me.'

She remembered the last time she'd sat in this café, tense and suspicious. As opposed to the last two days, when she'd laughed and talked and eaten and made love with Angus MacAllister to her heart's content.

In her favourite Shakespeare comedy, people were transformed because of fairies or love potions or a magical night in the woods. In her case, it had taken one wonderful weekend.

It was midsummer's day today, too, she realised. The twenty-first of June.

Of course, in a Shakespeare comedy, the play ended and the transformations were permanent. She wasn't sure that real life worked like that.

But for the length of a midsummer weekend's dream, she could believe it.

'I was afraid of you,' she said. 'I'm more like Jennifer than you think.'

He held one of the pastries up to her lips and she bit into it. It was flaky and sweet and it melted in her mouth.

'Well,' he said, 'I can understand that. I mean, it's not every day you meet a man who's hung like a—'

She nearly spit out her mouthful of pastry laughing.

'What?' He feigned shock. 'You mean that's not why you were afraid of me?'

She shook her head and swallowed. 'No. You reminded me of someone I had a relationship with.'

Angus sobered. 'Somebody who hurt you?'

'Hurt is an understatement.' She toyed with her coffee-cup. 'I was so in love with Robin that I couldn't see straight. And he was charming, like you. Arrogant.'

This time, Angus didn't make a joke about being arrogant. She was glad.

'He became quite a well-known actor, too, though he wasn't when we were together. He had that gift you have.' She gestured with her hands. 'Getting people to warm to him. Making them feel like they're the only person in the universe. It's very seductive. Even when it doesn't mean anything.'

Angus's brows drew together. 'You thought I was being insincere.'

'At first. And then not insincere, precisely, but…' She thought. 'In the end, it's hard to believe that somebody really cares for you when they seem to care for everybody. My parents were like that a little. They always had somebody new staying with us, or some new cause to go on marches about. The difference with them was that they made sure I knew they cared about me, too. Robin only seemed to care.'

'What did he do to you?'

She studied the pattern the froth and chocolate powder made on the side of her coffee-cup.

She wanted to tell him. As she'd wanted to tell him about Miss Wood and the oatmeal cookies. As if by magic, when she was with Angus, she was someone who shared her worries and her sorrows.

'I got pregnant,' she said. 'I was silly in love; I didn't care about the consequences. I forgot about birth control. When I told

Robin, he didn't want to know. He was far too interested in making new friends and finding new lovers.'

Angus's hand had crept to hers, as hers had to his when he'd been talking about his parents. 'And the baby?'

'I was going to go back to Canada to have it. I lost it at five months. So I stayed here.'

She heard him draw in a long breath and let it go. His hand tightened around hers. 'I'm sorry, Elisabeth.'

Even years after losing her baby, she didn't think she could look at the sympathy in his eyes. She stirred her coffee, crushing the foam.

'Anyway,' she said, 'it made me wary of good-looking charming men whom I'm ridiculously attracted to.'

He raised her hand to his lips and brushed a kiss across her knuckles. 'I'm not insincere, Elisabeth.'

'I know.' Or at least he didn't mean to be, which was almost the same thing. Deliberately, she made her voice light as she looked up into his face. 'You so deeply want to be liked that you chose a profession that exists purely to give others pleasure.'

Angus laughed. 'I never thought of it that way before. I thought it was because I was an inherent sensualist.'

'That too.'

He rubbed the back of her hand against his cheek; it was beginning to be rough with stubble since she'd watched him shave this morning. 'I've enjoyed being a sensualist with you this weekend.'

'Me too.' She picked up one of the pastries and fed him as he'd done to her, watching his strong white teeth, his tongue licking a crumb from his lips. 'You know, you never told us what your favourite food was, after you made us tell you.'

'That's easy. Soft-boiled eggs and toast soldiers.'

Elisabeth was so surprised she nearly dropped the pastry. 'That's it? No caviare or truffle oil or fancy Damien-Virata-style weirdness?'

'That's it. Hot slippery yolk and crunchy buttery toast. I love the feeling of cracking the egg open with my spoon. A little bit of salt sprinkled over it with my fingers. Brilliant.'

'I expected there to be some ice cream, at least.'

'Chocolate ice cream is a close second. But soft-boiled eggs and toast soldiers are the only thing I can remember anyone making just for me when I was a kid.'

His face looked so wistful and lonely for a moment that Elisabeth leaned over the table and kissed him on the lips. Wanting to take that loneliness away.

She tasted pastry and coffee and Angus and with the kiss she remembered all the other kisses they'd shared this weekend. Swift and stolen, walking along the road hand in hand; laughing, teasing on his couch; slow and passionate while water sluiced over their bodies in the shower. The first one, a gentle touching in the cold.

And after all that kissing, all the times they'd made love, explored, learned each other, she still wanted more.

Her tongue touched his and she heard him moan deep in his throat. She remembered his gravelly voice shouting out her name. The driving intensity in his body at his climax.

'I want you,' she whispered when they broke apart.

'Race you back to my house.'

She glanced over his shoulder and saw the afternoon had gone dark. Rain poured down outside the windows. She realised she'd been hearing its sound for a while, without listening to it.

'It's raining,' she said.

'Even better. I love it when you're wet.'

The sexy *double entendre* shot another pang of desire through her. She pushed back her chair and ran to the door of the café. '*Ciao,* Luciano!' she called and burst through the door into the wet air, leaving Angus behind her still reaching for his wallet.

The rain was cool on her bare legs as she ran, and plastered Angus's shirt to her body. She was more than halfway to his house before he caught up with her.

'That wasn't fair,' he gasped, grabbing her by the waist from behind.

'It's not only ex-public schoolboys who can play dirty.' She tried to hook her leg around his, to trip him up, but he deftly avoided her.

'I certainly hope that's true.' He pulled her to the side and behind him, and sprinted ahead.

She didn't have a chance of catching up with his long-legged, athletic stride, but she tried her best anyway in her little dress and her beaded shoes. By the time she climbed the steps to his door she was breathless, soaked to the skin, and he was already un-locking the door.

She pushed underneath his arm and fell through the door ahead of him just as he opened it.

'Yes! Beat you!' she cried.

He put his arms around her and marched her backwards to the living room. 'You're adorable when you cheat.'

He kissed her passionately and Elisabeth tore at the buttons of his shirt. The wet cotton parted under her hands and she exposed his chest, ran her hands over the hardness of his ribs, the different hardness of his stomach muscles, the thin trail of wiry hair that led down to the waistband of his trousers.

Angus peeled off the shirt she wore and reached round to unzip her dress. Wet, it clung to her, and he had to push it over her shoulders and down her body. She stepped out of it on the way backwards to the couch.

Then they fell onto the cushions together, Angus on top of her, kissing the whole time. She fumbled with his belt, her fingers clumsy with need, suddenly so urgent she couldn't stand it. His lips were on her throat, his hands pushing down her bra to free her breasts, pulling down her damp knickers. She got his belt unfastened and his jeans and they were too wet to get rid of easily, so she made a frustrated noise in her throat and he laughed and reached down and took them off.

She wrapped her fingers around his penis. She loved the feel of him, hot and heavy and velvet-skinned. 'Condom,' she panted. 'I want you now.'

He dipped into his jeans pocket and rolled on the condom with deft fingers and she reached for him impatiently and pulled him to her. With a single strong thrust he was inside her, filling her. He let out a long groan. Elisabeth wrapped her legs around him and dug her fingers into his back.

Faster. Harder. She urged him with her panting breaths, her mouth devouring his, to be wilder, to lose control. He pounded into her and Elisabeth felt her mind slip away, felt herself become a hunger racing towards satisfaction. Felt them growing closer, running together, even faster now.

He tilted her hips so he plunged even deeper, she heard their bodies moving together, his flesh against hers, she gulped in ragged breaths full of Angus and it had only been minutes, seconds, but her orgasm sizzled through her and she screamed a wordless cry into his mouth, clamped down on him with her entire body and pulled him with her.

Angus collapsed on top of her, pressing kisses to her lips, her cheeks, her forehead damp with sweat. He was heavy and hot and wonderful on her.

'Wow,' he gasped. 'I think Luciano should market his coffee as an aphrodisiac.'

'No, it's you that's the aphrodisiac.' All of her body tingled, languid and happy.

'I think it's you. I can't get enough of you.' He kissed her again, tenderly after their wild passion, and rolled so he was on his side next to her. She sighed and closed her eyes, letting herself drift away into contentment.

'Oh.'

There was something in his voice that made her open her eyes. Angus sat up, his broad back to her.

'Angus? What's wrong?'

He didn't answer her right away, and she struggled up onto her knees beside him. 'What is it, Angus?'

His eyebrows were drawn down, his face concerned as he looked at her. 'I'm sorry, sweetheart. The condom split.'

She took it all in at once: the condom in his hand, Angus's dismay. It hit her like a wall of dread.

'Hey.' Angus put the condom aside and wrapped his arms around her. 'Elisabeth, I am so sorry.'

Sorry. He was sorry. That he'd had unprotected sex with her.

'It's not your fault,' she said automatically to his naked chest. 'These things happen.'

'Yes, but after what you were telling me about what you went through. I didn't want this.' He kissed the top of her head and held her tight.

'It's okay,' she said. But it wasn't.

He pulled her apart from him to look into her face. 'I'm safe, Elisabeth. I don't sleep around. I'm healthy.'

She nodded. Safe. The word echoed through her numbed brain.

She'd thought she'd be safe with him for a weekend. She'd thought she could live for the present, not worry about the future.

And with a single careless action, a single stupid torn condom, they'd maybe determined the future of the rest of their lives.

For no reason other than pleasure.

'I'd better go and wash,' she said and disengaged herself from him. She felt him watching her as she stood and picked up her underwear and her dress from the floor. They were paltry covering but she held them up against her as she left the living room and climbed the stairs to the master bedroom and its *en suite* bathroom.

She turned the shower on and stepped in. Hot water didn't make her feel any better. She remembered being in this shower with Angus, him holding her strong against the tiled walls, him washing her gently afterwards.

All pleasure. Meaning nothing. Sensations, nerve endings, pheromones.

Elisabeth twisted the tap to cold. The drops hit her like needles but when she came out of the shower she felt no more numb than she had going in.

She dried herself and folded the towel on the rail. She brushed her wet hair using Angus's hairbrush. Carefully she picked out the loose hairs she'd left in his brush and dropped them in the bin. Her dress was wrinkled and damp but she put it on, smoothing it with her hands.

When she came out into the bedroom Angus was there, putting on a dry pair of jeans and a fresh shirt. He frowned when he saw her. 'You shouldn't be wearing those wet clothes,' he said.

'It's fine.' She overtly checked his alarm clock beside his bed.

'It's getting late, Angus, and I've got a lot of work to do at home for school tomorrow.'

He looked at the clock. 'It's not six yet. You've got plenty of time. It's the longest day of the year.'

'And I have a lot of work.' She picked up her high-heeled shoes from the floor near the bed and lifted her green glass necklace from the bedside table.

'Elisabeth—' He stepped towards her with his hand outstretched. She didn't take it.

'I came for a weekend, Angus. The weekend's over. And I need to get home.'

He held out his hand for a moment more, then dropped it.

'I'll drive you,' he said.

She nodded and went downstairs. Her handbag was in the hallway and her beaded shoes were flung on the carpet where she'd dropped them. She slid them on her feet, realised they were wet, and put on her heels instead. She put her necklace into her bag. It looked less bright now that *Be here now* was over.

She looked around the living room for anything else of hers. Angus had straightened the couch, disposed of the damaged condom, taken away the clothes she'd torn off him.

There was nothing here connected to her. Besides her hair in the bin and her fingerprints on the shiny surfaces, she'd left no trace of herself in the house. She'd entered with nothing more than her handbag and the clothes she stood in. She was taking all that with her.

And maybe something more.

She could take the morning-after pill, she thought, and immediately knew that, no, she couldn't.

She'd lost a baby. She couldn't get rid of one, even if it were only a chance for one. Even if it were unplanned, again, the result of a mistake.

Elisabeth stood by the door until Angus came down the stairs. 'I wish I were welcoming you in instead of taking you home,' he said, snagging his car keys from a bowl on the hall table and opening the door for her, and she could tell he was making his voice sound light and charming intentionally.

It had stopped raining and the streets were wet and shining in the sun. His car was parked around the corner from his house. It was a glossy low-slung classic Jaguar, impeccably restored. 'I see what Danny was impressed about,' she said, trying to match his carefree tone.

'It's a nineteen sixty-seven E-type, series one.' He opened the door for her and then walked around the long bonnet to get in himself.

Leather upholstery, soft as butter. When he started the engine it purred, vibrating the seat beneath Elisabeth. The sense of restrained power was palpable as he pulled away from the kerb.

A very expensive car, chosen, no doubt, for its sensual impact. Typical.

In sharp contrast to the weekend, which had gone far too quickly, the drive to her flat took far too long. She stared at London going by through the windscreen, giving him directions to her flat. As she lived near the school, she didn't have to say much.

'What are you teaching tomorrow?' he asked after a stretch of silence.

She outlined her lesson plans for the day, but she knew he wasn't really listening. She wasn't really listening, either. She wanted to get home, to leave him, and she also wanted him to turn the car around and drive back to an hour ago when they'd truly been together.

He pulled up in front of the large Edwardian building that contained her flat. He pulled on the handbrake and turned the key in the ignition. With the engine off, the stillness between them seemed even greater.

'Going to invite me in?' His usual cheeky smile.

'I don't think watching me marking coursework will be very much fun for you. Besides, I know you put off a lot to be with me this weekend. You must have loads of work to catch up with.'

'I do. But I'd rather be with you.'

She tsked. 'That's not the attitude that's going to get you a third Michelin star, Mr MacAllister.' She leaned over and kissed him on the cheek. It was slightly rough with the beginning of stubble, and it smelled exactly as it had not an hour ago when he'd been inside her, her hips in his hands, kissing her and making love to her as if she were the most desirable woman in the universe.

'Thank you for a wonderful weekend,' she said and opened up the car door.

'Elisabeth—'

She pretended not to hear him and shut the door. As she walked up the pavement to her door she focused on finding her keys in her handbag and not looking back at him. The Jag was quiet, and she knew he was watching her.

She unlocked her door and looked back over her shoulder. He had wound down the passenger-side window. He waved to her.

She faked a smile, waved back, and went inside, up the stairs to her flat. Midsummer's day, and another four hours of daylight ahead of her, even though the dream was over.

## CHAPTER TEN

THE bell rang for the end of the school day. As usual, her year sevens' faces lit up with joy at the sound.

Elisabeth's stomach sank.

If the day was over, she had to go home. If she had to go home, she had to start thinking.

Maybe she could give somebody detention and stay for another half an hour. But as soon as she thought of it, she knew she couldn't be so unfair. She sat down in her chair and watched her students pack up.

'Alison, please push your chair in,' she said automatically. 'Karim, could you pick up that piece of paper from the floor, please? Jay, remember you're redoing that piece of work for me tomorrow. Have a good evening, everybody.'

The students said goodbye to her as they filed out the door, their backpacks in several instances nearly as big as they were. She sat back in her chair and closed her eyes.

'Miss?'

She opened her eyes to see little Jimmy Peto, freckle-faced, cowlick-haired.

'Yes, Jimmy?'

'Do you think you could bring in a chicken to English some time, like that chef guy did in our food technology class? That was mental.'

'I don't think chickens have much to do with English literature, Jimmy.'

'Well, maybe we could read something about chickens, yeah?

Or maybe some other animals instead of this Shakespeare stuff. I've got a guinea pig I could bring in some-time if you wanted.'

She shook her head. 'I'd love to see your guinea pig but I don't think it's a good idea to bring it in to school. It would probably be scared.'

'Not my guinea pig, miss. She's tough. She bit my dog one time.' Jimmy's thoughts flitted across his face like fluffy clouds against a sunshiny sky. 'I wish Angus MacAllister would teach us again in food technology. He was cool. Not like Miss Cutter, who keeps on making us make things with alfalfa sprouts.' He stuck out his tongue.

'Maybe he'll come back one day to teach you. Have a good evening, Jimmy.'

'You too, miss.' Jimmy hefted his backpack and wobbled out of the room.

He passed Jennifer, who was on her way in. Next to Jimmy, she looked tall. Or maybe that was because she wasn't hanging her head.

She stood by Elisabeth's desk and held out a piece of paper. 'Will you look at my menu?' she asked. 'I've been going through it and I've been trying to figure out if I can get everything done in the time I'll have for the competition. I mean, I can make some things beforehand, like stock, but I'm not sure.'

Elisabeth took the paper, which was covered with crossings-out and corrections. 'You've got chicken soup as a starter,' she observed. 'With noodles.'

Jennifer blushed but nodded. 'I've been practising making fresh pasta. But I'm not sure I can do that and make a mousse too, because they both need doing before I start the main course. I mean, I only have two weeks to practise before the contest. What do you think?'

Elisabeth wondered if Jennifer had ever had the courage to ask someone else for help.

'I don't know, Jennifer,' she said gently; 'I'm good at sonnets and spelling, but I'm not much of a cook. This is probably some-thing you should ask Miss Cutter. Or Angus.'

Funny how she could say his name like that, so normally, so much as if he weren't the first and last and only thing she was thinking about.

'I'll ask Angus.' Jennifer, however, pronounced his name with a quiet relish, a pride. 'Do you like him, Miss Read?'

The question was quick and unexpected—from the look on Jennifer's face, it had surprised her, too.

'Yes,' Elisabeth said, 'I do. You do too, don't you, Jennifer?'

The girl nodded. 'I don't think Danny's noticed though.'

Elisabeth was puzzled by this for a moment before she realised that Jennifer was using a fifteen-year-old girl's definition of the word 'like', meaning to fancy, to want to go out with, and that she was reassuring her teacher that Danny hadn't detected the crush both the female members of their quartet had on Angus MacAllister.

Jennifer picked up her paper. 'I'm glad he got me to learn how to make chicken soup. Bye, Miss Read.'

'See you later, Jennifer.'

Angus MacAllister. Everywhere she went, she was reminded of the effect he had on people's lives. The transformation he'd started in Jennifer was nothing short of miraculous.

And the transformation he'd started in her...

Elisabeth shook her head firmly. That transformation had been a temporary madness. Nothing to do with her normal life. She gathered her things together to leave school. When she unlocked her desk drawer to take out her handbag she turned on her mobile phone. But there were no messages. He hadn't rung her.

Why should he? she thought as she left the school, threading through crowds of students waiting for the bus. He'd invited her for a weekend together and that weekend was over. They didn't have any reason to see each other again until Wednesday, their regularly scheduled session with the kids. Angus was busy, she was busy, they both had lives and jobs and other people to spend time with, and something silly like a split condom, which probably wouldn't matter anyway, didn't change—

Her phone rang. She stopped in the middle of the pavement and dug inside her bag, her fingers hasty and numb. She didn't recognise the number on the screen but she didn't know Angus's number anyway.

She forced herself to clear her throat before she answered. 'Hello?'

'Hello, is this Elisabeth Read?'

Not Angus. The disappointment felt as if someone had seized her stomach and twisted it.

'Yes, who's calling?'

'You don't know me, Elisabeth, but my name is Clive Jones, and I was given your number.'

The man's voice had a definite Welsh lilt, and Elisabeth realised who it must be: the tango-dancing Welshman Jo was trying to set her up with.

The last thing she needed right now was a date. Still, he was a friend of Joanna's. 'Oh, yes, I know. Thanks for calling, Clive. How are you?'

'I'm fine, thank you, Elisabeth. Actually I was wondering if you and I could get together, maybe this afternoon, for a drink? I'm hoping school's over for the day?'

'It is, but as a matter of fact, Clive, I—'

'I know you're busy but really I just want to meet you, talk with you for a few minutes. I won't mind if that's all. Honest. I'm in the neighbourhood, you see, which is why I called, so I thought maybe we could meet at Benny's. It's near your school, I think, and you could pop in on your way home, for a quick drink with me?'

He certainly was insistent. Knowing Jo, she'd talked Elisabeth up. Benny's was right round the corner; it would be more polite to meet with him and tell him face to face that she wasn't interested in dating him.

And what better thing did she have to do, anyway?

'All right,' she said. 'How will I know you?'

'Don't worry,' he said, and he sounded so pleased that she felt guilty that she'd be giving him the brush-off in ten minutes. 'I'll know you. I'm at Benny's now, so I'll see you in a few minutes.'

She tucked the phone back into her handbag and headed towards the wine bar.

It was well lit, nearly empty at this time of the afternoon. A man sitting at a table near the door rose as soon as she entered and approached her, his hand outstretched.

'Elisabeth? It's Clive. Thanks for agreeing to meet me.'

'It's nice to meet you, Clive.' He was slight, shorter than she was, with thin blond hair. Not her type at all. She wondered what Jo had been thinking.

Maybe he was a really good dancer.

'What would you like to drink?'

She asked for a mineral water and watched Clive go up to the bar. She should have asked for a coffee. She'd hardly slept last night; she'd felt tense as a violin string. And her bed had felt empty.

Impossible as it seemed, after only two nights she'd become used to sleeping in Angus's arms.

Then again, after the day she'd had, she felt too jumpy for caffeine. She probably should have a glass of wine and try to relax.

*Except you shouldn't drink if you're pregnant,* a voice in the back of her head said.

Clive returned with a tall glass of water for her and a pint of lager for himself. As he sat across from her she wondered what on earth she was doing sitting in a wine bar across from a man when there was a possibility she might be carrying Angus's baby.

'I'm sorry, Clive,' she blurted. 'I know I told Joanna you should call me for a date but I don't think it's a good idea.'

Clive seemed surprised. Of course he would be—she wasn't exactly handling this tactfully.

'I mean, you seem like a nice guy and Joanna has only praise for you, but I—'

'You're seeing someone else,' he finished for her.

Not any more. 'Well, yes.'

He nodded. 'It's a new thing, I take it. He swept you off your feet before I could get to you, huh?'

'Something like that. I'm sorry, Clive. I didn't mean to lead you on but I thought I should meet with you and tell you in person.'

Clive took a long pull of his beer. 'Well, it's a disappointment, Elisabeth, but I'm glad you're being honest with me.' He put his beer down and leaned on the table. 'Is he really that special? Any chance of you dumping him for me?'

'He's very talented,' she said carefully, toying with her glass.

'Is this a fling, do you think, or are you thinking marriage, children, all that sort of stuff?'

Marriage then children. That was the order she'd wanted to

go about it. She shifted in her seat, uncomfortable with having to keep up this charade of being in a happy new relationship.

'Oh, it's early for that.'

'You've got enough of kids at school?'

'No, I want children, eventually.'

Wanted children? She ached for them. Every time she saw a baby, she thought of the one she'd lost, thought about the ones she would some day have.

Being pregnant with Angus's child was not a good idea. If she had her choice, she wouldn't choose to be a single mother. But she'd come to terms with that possibility last time she was pregnant, and she knew she could do it if she had to. Because in the end, a child mattered more than a wedding ring. Although she'd always wanted to do things differently from her parents, they'd given her a loving home, even if they hadn't been married. She could do that, too.

Enough. 'So how did you get into tango dancing?' she asked, to change the subject.

He was mid-sip of his beer and he suddenly snorted, spilling it over the lip of his glass.

'Oh, I don't know,' he sputtered. 'Just fell into it, I guess.'

What a strange answer. How did you fall into tango dancing? And why would the question make him laugh?

'Anyway, enough about me,' he said. 'Tell me some more about yourself.'

Elisabeth pushed back her chair. She couldn't figure out why Joanna had thought she'd be interested in this guy; he was getting odder by the second. Maybe Jo had met him on a good day. To be fair, Elisabeth wasn't at her best, either.

'I'm sorry, Clive, but I've got to be going now.' She stood. He stood too.

'Are you sure? I was really enjoying talking with you.'

'I'm sure. It was very nice to meet you, though.' She held out her hand and he shook it.

'Good luck with your new bloke, Elisabeth.'

'Thanks.' *Not sure luck has anything to do with it,* she thought, and left Clive and the wine bar.

She would spend this evening thinking about her marking, she told herself on her way home. She would catch up with everything she hadn't done this weekend. And she'd turn off her phone, so she wouldn't be expecting it to ring. Because it wouldn't.

She reached into her bag and got out her phone and turned it off as she turned the corner to her road.

And then she looked up, and she stopped.

In front of her building: a red nineteen sixty-seven, E-type, Series 1 Jaguar. With Angus MacAllister leaning against it.

He saw her the same moment she saw him, and he smiled. Elisabeth's stomach flipped over.

How had she walked away from him yesterday?

'Elisabeth,' he said and covered the distance between them and took her in his arms.

She breathed him deep. And understood what that ache had been inside her all day, because it disappeared.

'I've missed you,' he said.

'Don't be silly, it hasn't even been a day since we've seen each other,' she said to his shoulder. Knowing she was pretending.

He relaxed his hold on her a little bit and tilted up her chin with one hand. 'Sensible Miss Read.'

'Well, it hasn't. And I'm sure you've been busy.'

'I've been at Magnum all day. They were fine without me this weekend.'

'I'm so sorry. It must be terrible to find out you're not as important as you thought.'

He grinned down at her. 'You're afraid I'm going to charm you again, aren't you?'

'Yes.'

'I don't blame you, because that's exactly what I've come here to do.'

And he was doing it already. Her hands wanted to creep underneath his suit jacket, unbutton his shirt, feel all the textures of his chest. 'If you expected me to swoon at your feet just because of your flash car, you can forget it. I've seen it already.'

'Curses. There goes my nefarious master plan. I looked for you at school first, but I was too late. Have you come from there?'

'More or less.'

'Have you eaten?'

'Not since lunch.'

'Perfect.' He let her go, opened his car door, and took out an insulated box.

'What's that?'

'Nefarious Master Plan B. Can I come in?'

It had been a foregone conclusion from the moment she'd seen him again. 'Yes.'

'Brilliant.' He reached in his car again and took out a bottle wrapped in a silver insulated sleeve, then bumped the door shut with his hip and balanced the bottle on top of the box to lock the car door. Every movement deft and sure.

He followed her up the stairs to her flat. He felt very close, their footsteps echoing together in the cool stairwell. She opened the door and they went inside.

Her flat was substantially smaller than his house. Angus, standing in her living room, seemed to take up a lot of space— not just because of his tallness, but because of his energy, his presence. She saw him take in the plain furniture with its rich embroidered pillows and crocheted throws, the walls lined with books, the houseplants that clustered around the windows.

He put down his box and his bottle on the coffee-table and stroked one of his fingers down the lush green leaf of one of her plants. 'You're a nurturer,' he said.

'It's not me, it's the poetry I read aloud to them. They particularly like Keats and old Bob Dylan lyrics.'

He let go of the leaf. 'You've got your defences up so high I think I might need a ladder.'

Even the air felt different in her flat with him in it. And he was surprised she was defending herself? 'What's in the box?'

He took off the lid and pulled out a succession of plastic take-away containers, naming their contents one by one. 'Ravioli of Scottish lobster and langoustine, poached in lobster bisque. Duck confit, blood orange, white turnips and *foie gras* sauce. And most of a lemon tart.' He peeled up the cover of one of the boxes and examined what was in it. 'The presentation isn't great, but then again these boxes were designed for chicken chow mein.'

She stared. 'You brought all this from Magnum? As a take-away?'

'Domino's doesn't do lobster. Have you got some plates? And some glasses?' He produced a corkscrew from his jacket pocket and opened the bottle with quick, economical movements.

She shook her head incredulously and went to fetch place-mats, napkins, plates, glasses, and cutlery. When she returned Angus took the stack of plates from her and set the coffee-table and then opened two of the containers and within seconds had reassembled concoctions of ravioli, sauce, and garnish on the plates. A rich smell filled the room, and Elisabeth realised her mouth was watering.

Whether that was because of the food, or because of Angus's focused competence while he prepared it, she wasn't sure.

She sat down on the couch. 'Wine?' Angus asked. He held the bottle poised over her glass.

'No, thank you.'

He put down the bottle and sat next to her. 'Elisabeth,' he said. 'I know you're thinking there's a possibility you could be pregnant.'

'It's probably fine. The chances are so small. I'm sure it will be okay.' And she'd just said the same thing three times. She couldn't be more unconvincing if she tried.

He took her hand in his. 'You're worried, and I can't blame you. But, Elisabeth, if you were pregnant, I would not do the same thing that Robin did to you.'

Her eyes burned; she blinked hard. 'It's not going to happen so it's irrelevant.'

'It might happen. And you need to know that if it did, you wouldn't be alone. I would stay with you, I would stay with the baby, we would be together. Look at me, Elisabeth.'

She looked at him. His grey eyes were steady, serious.

He'd said it several times. Protested too much. But, unlike her, he sounded completely sincere.

Angus was good at sounding sincere. She was sure it was a skill he'd perfected over the years, another weapon in his arsenal of charm.

'This isn't what you signed on for when you asked me to spend the weekend with you,' she said.

'No, it wasn't. And we tried to avoid it. But if it happens, we'll make the best of it. Okay?'

He squeezed her hand and she searched his face. There was a line of concentration on his forehead, and no hint of a smile on his lips.

He was a man used to getting his own way, a man used to independence and pleasure. Most importantly, he was a man who centred his entire life around making people like him, saying the thing that people wanted to hear.

He might mean something very different when he had to take care of a baby he hadn't wanted.

But for now, he was convinced that he was telling the truth, as he believed it.

She nodded. Angus's face broke into a smile. He reached over and pulled her into his lap.

So close to his body, her face next to his clean-shaven, lemony-smelling skin. She saw the whorl of his ear, the small smile lines near his mouth, how his dark hair just touched his collar at the back. Every detail was exquisite, exciting, dear to her.

'I've thought about you every minute we haven't been together,' he murmured. 'I've been dying to touch you and talk to you. I nearly drove over and burst into one of your lessons but I was afraid I'd get banned from the school.'

'If you'd brought in MacNugget again you would've assured your popularity for life.'

'I didn't want to play show and tell with a chicken. I wanted to abduct the teacher and sweep her away and make love to her.'

His words sent a shudder through her, made her entire body want to melt into his. Made her recognise, at last, the truth about this situation.

She could worry about the future and his sincerity and being pregnant all she wanted. But the pure reality was that Elisabeth wanted Angus so badly that none of those worries made a blind bit of difference.

She wound her fingers in his hair and kissed him. His wonderful, sensual, talented, charming mouth. She let herself taste him, lose herself in his body and his pure joy at life. And she knew she'd wanted to do this every second she'd been away from him.

He shifted her slightly on his lap and she felt his arousal against her thigh, proof that his passion was as volatile as hers. Her fingers desperate, she began to unbutton his shirt, pushed her hands inside to feel his naked skin while he slipped his own hands up beneath her top to hold her breasts.

'Our take-away's going to go cold, isn't it?' she said, and then gasped as he teased her nipples with his thumbs through her bra.

'That,' he said, pressing kisses down her throat, 'is exactly what I hoped would happen when I brought it here.'

'Nefarious Plan C,' she agreed.

He manoeuvred her so that she was facing him, her legs around his waist, and pulled her up snug against him. Even through their layers of clothes she could feel the length and heat of his erection between her legs. She remembered all the pleasure they could give each other. How he felt hard and slick, pounding into her, the scent of his body musky with sweat.

Angus looked down into her face. He touched the corner of her eye with the tip of one finger, the place where her tears would have fallen if she'd let them.

'Don't shut me out,' he said to her. 'I can't bear it.'

So, so tempting to believe. She pushed herself still closer to him and covered his face with kisses. Rubbed her lips over his eyebrows: rough velvet.

'I can't resist you, Angus,' she whispered. She tested the lobe of his ear between her teeth, such a tender morsel on such a strong man, and heard him groan.

Sex, between them, had its own reality, built its own world that she could believe in.

She slid off his lap onto her knees on the carpet before him, and looked up into his face with eyes she knew were as mischievous as his own could be.

'I'm very hungry,' she said, and slid his belt from its loops.

# CHAPTER ELEVEN

'ABSOLUTELY brilliant.'

The Angus on television grinned at the camera and raised his glass of wine in a toast as the credits rolled.

Christine hit 'off' on the remote. 'It's a fantastic series, Angus. Funny, stylish, sexy. The camera loves you. This one's going to send the ratings through the roof.'

The real Angus slumped in his chair, arms crossed over his chest. 'I don't like it.'

She stared in surprise. 'You're joking. It's even better than your last series. The production is great, the food looks amazing, the music is trendy. What is there not to like?'

He got up and poured them each a coffee from the pot on the table of the boardroom. 'I don't like myself.'

'What do you mean?'

'Have I always been—' he gestured at the blank television '—like that? Always smiling, talking fast? Superficial?'

'It's your public image, Angus. It's a TV show, not an anatomy of your soul.'

'I know.' He sat back down and slid her coffee over to her. 'The thing is, I don't know if there's much difference between the TV show and who I really am.'

Christine looked hard at him. 'You're becoming very introspective these days, Angus. Aren't you happy?'

He thought about it. His restaurant was the most popular it had ever been, he was very good at a job he loved, he'd spent the last five weeks really helping some kids, and for the past week he had repeatedly had the best sex of his life with a woman he thought was wonderful in every way.

He should be happy.

He looked at his watch and pushed back his chair. 'I'm going to be late for the kids.'

Christine was watching him with concern. 'Do you want me to do something about the show?'

'No.' He picked up two heavy carrier bags near the door. 'The show will be fine. And you can't do anything about who I am. Thanks, Christine.'

Outside the studio he hailed a cab to the school. As he watched Soho slip away into Piccadilly, he remembered what Elisabeth had said last Sunday in Luciano's.

*You so deeply want to be liked that you chose a profession that exists purely to give others pleasure.*

Was that really what he was about? Pleasure? Trying desperately all the time to be liked?

That was how he'd appeared on TV, he thought grimly. It had been a shock to see it—even more so because he'd seen himself on television plenty of times before, and never noticed it. He'd always liked how his TV shows turned out.

Maybe he'd been satisfied with pleasure and being liked before. But something had definitely changed. Because Elisabeth Read liked him, and the two of them over the past seven days had shared more pleasure than he'd believed possible.

But that wasn't enough.

He banged his fist on the cab door.

He'd been happy with Elisabeth. On that first weekend she'd been open, laughing, honest, herself. She'd met his eyes every time she'd talked with him.

And she'd been that way in the five days since, at times. At moments when she'd tell him a funny story about her odd upbringing, or confide about a child she was worried about at school. Or when he caught her looking at him when she didn't think he could see.

And always, always when they were making love. Then, she was open with him, frank with her pleasures and her desires, surprising him with her depth and the emotion he could see in her face.

But other times, she had her defences up as high as they could go. She'd be teasing him, laughing, but he could see she wasn't there. She was lost in some private thought, some private doubt, and she wouldn't let him in. It had been that way as soon as the condom had split. The shutters had come down with a clang, and she hadn't raised them fully since.

Was that his fault? Was it because in reality he was exactly as he appeared on TV: a people-pleaser, someone who charmed and laughed and stayed on the surface of things?

Who were his close friends? Everybody he knew liked him. But who went deeper than that?

He frowned at the cars passing the other way, and saw his reflection in the window. He didn't have time to have close friends; he'd been working like a man possessed since he was an apprentice at sixteen. He'd had to. He'd refused his parents' money, started at the bottom, forged everything he had with his own hands.

The cab stopped at the gates of Elisabeth's school and he got out and paid the driver. There were a lot fewer kids than there normally were when he arrived, and when he looked at his watch he saw he was nearly twenty minutes late.

He swore and ran to Reception lugging the heavy bags. Danny and Jennifer were doing a trial run for the competition today, creating their menus in timed conditions without any help, and they couldn't start without the ingredients he'd promised them.

A few words with Harjeet and a guest badge on his lapel, and he was running through the now-familiar school corridors to the food technology room.

When he arrived Jennifer and Elisabeth were talking quietly at one end of the room and Danny had spread his ingredients out all over his work space.

'Hey, Angus!' Danny greeted him loudly. 'You're late, man!'

The smile Elisabeth sent him across the room kicked at his heart. He loved the quiet camaraderie she'd forged with little Jennifer. She was so kind and careful with the girl. He remembered Elisabeth's touch on his own hand when he'd told her about his lonely childhood.

'Sorry, mate, I was watching my next TV series, lost track of the time.'

As soon as he said it he was mentally slapping himself. Did he really want to teach Danny that success was public attention?

'Wicked!' the boy cried.

'No, it was irresponsible. I should have been here on time. I expect Miss Read will tell me off.' He put his carrier bags on the table and handed bottles and packages to Jennifer and Danny. 'And you'd better get on with it if we're going to finish before midnight. I'm starting the timer in five minutes.'

'Yes, Chef,' the students said and hurried to their workspaces to arrange their ingredients and equipment.

Elisabeth came to his side, touched his arm secretly. 'You're in trouble.'

'I intend to take my punishment like a man,' he said. 'As long as it's you giving it to me.'

'Do you think they'll get everything done on time?' she asked him. 'There's only a week until the competition. I'm worried that we should've practised all of this before.'

He welcomed the serious question. 'It's a balance. We want them to be confident, but we don't want to practise so many times that they get bored.'

'I don't think Jennifer would get bored. She has a lot of discipline, that girl, though she doesn't show it.'

'Danny would. He's good, but he loses focus if he hasn't got somebody standing over him, and there will be a lot of distractions at the competition. I want him to know what he's doing but not be able to go into autopilot.' He watched the kids checking through their ingredients. 'The practice runs next week will be useful, but I think they'll be ready by Saturday.'

'It's just that it's so important for them.' She bit her lip. He looked at the indentation her teeth made, and wanted to press his own mouth to it.

'Yes, but we want it to be fun, too. They're kids.'

'Trust you to put fun first,' she said, and her tone was teasing, but it got him.

Putting fun first. That was what she thought of him. It wasn't surprising she didn't trust him.

He picked up a plastic timer and set it for two hours. 'All right, kids, time to get to work. Remember, you're doing all this yourself. Miss Read and I will be watching but we won't be doing anything except for washing up. It's your show now. Ready?'

'Yes, Chef,' both of them answered, and he started the timer. They immediately got to work.

'I'm not all fun and games, you know,' he said to Elisabeth.

She smiled at him. 'Whatever you say, Chef.'

It was always difficult not to hold her and kiss her when the children were around. He wondered if Elisabeth would ever think it was appropriate to show affection at school. He understood why she wouldn't want to involve the children in her private life. But it seemed so unnatural not to slip his arm around her waist, push her glossy hair back with his fingers.

Of course she wouldn't want him to touch her in public, at her place of work, if she only saw their relationship as a fling.

He prowled the kitchen watching the kids. Jennifer was sure-handed, thorough, careful. Danny made a mistake, swore under his breath, and then did it perfectly.

Angus felt irritable and impatient, as if he'd had too much caffeine and sugar, but he did his best to hide it. He praised them quietly, offered no advice, though he saw Danny working over too high a flame and Jennifer mistiming her pasta. He bit back the orders he wanted to give. They'd learn from their errors, just as he had. Just as he was trying to do now.

*Trust me!* he wanted to tell Elisabeth. *Tell me what you're thinking!* And he wanted her to reply, *Yes, Chef,* and magically be the real Elisabeth again.

Why couldn't he enjoy the good things they had together? Why was he constantly wanting more than she gave him?

What was *wrong* with him?

Jennifer was making a velouté and even from halfway across the room he could see it was about to curdle. He pressed his mouth closed and turned on a hot-water tap, squeezed some frothy liquid into the basin and put the dishes and equipment he'd gathered into it.

Years of working in a kitchen and he was doing the washing up. Years of being an adult and he still couldn't figure out his own emotions. He scrubbed a pan and banged it onto the draining-board.

As he was washing the next thing he looked up. Elisabeth was directly across from him, watching Jennifer.

The velouté curdled. He heard Jennifer's quiet sound of dismay. And saw Elisabeth's face, so full of support and encouragement, fall. As if she felt everything Jennifer felt, as if she were the velouté herself.

She cared so, so much.

And he loved her.

At the thought, his hands fumbled underneath the water, and the knife that he was holding slipped. A sharp knife, as he'd taught them. So sharp, he understood its slice before he registered the pain in his left thumb.

He swore. The water turned pink much more quickly than he expected.

Danny, Jennifer, and Elisabeth were around him in an instant. 'Are you all right?' Elisabeth asked, and she blanched when she saw the sink full of water, blood-coloured now.

'Yes. Danny, Jennifer, get back to your work. You haven't got a lot of time left.'

Obediently, they left him. Elisabeth stayed.

'First-aid kit is by the door,' he told her. He wrapped his fist around his thumb and watched her. Slender, tall, and every inch of her body focused upon making life better for others.

He was so in love with her that he'd give up every single thing he had achieved just to have her love him back.

'Angus, sit down,' she said when she returned with the kit. 'You're as white as a sheet.' She took him by the elbow, as if she were the stronger of the two, and guided him to a chair. 'You're bleeding like crazy. What did you do?'

'I dropped a knife. I'm fine.' He looked down and was surprised to see blood dripping from his fist. He opened his hand

and heard Elisabeth's sharp intake of breath at the sight of the long slice down the pad of his thumb.

'I think we need to get you to a hospital,' she said.

'No need. I've had worse.' He took a roll of cotton wool from her and bound it tightly around his thumb. Blood bloomed through it immediately. He wound it thick and gave the end of it to her to cut.

Her movements were careful. She bit her lip in concern. He loved her and she might be carrying his baby.

Finished cutting, she glanced up and her forehead furrowed. 'Angus, you're looking at me very strangely. I think you're in shock.'

'A little bit,' he said. 'But it's a good sort of shock.'

Her frown deepened. 'Right. I'm taking you to a hospital. I don't like the way you're acting.'

If he didn't talk fast, he was going to end up explaining to a doctor that he was lovesick.

'No. I'm fine, Elisabeth. I've done this a few times before, remember? I don't need stitches and I'm not going to faint. And, besides, the kids need us here.'

She gazed at him, considering.

Did she love him? Could she love him? What could he do to make her love him?

'All right,' she said finally, 'but if that doesn't stop bleeding soon we're going no matter what you say.'

'I love it when you get all authoritative with me.'

That, apparently, was typical enough so that she relaxed a little and sat down on a chair beside him. 'You're having an off-day today—first you were late, and now you've cut yourself.'

'It has been a very unusual day,' he agreed. 'I'm going to have to be more careful.'

He'd have to take it slowly, build up trust between them. If he told her he loved her out of the blue, she wouldn't believe him. He could lose her.

He waited until both of the kids were wholly focused on their cooking, and he caressed the soft skin of her cheek with his un-injured hand, savoured the way she leaned into his palm just for a moment before discretion demanded he take his hand away.

She was so precious. And he'd never convinced anybody to love him before. He'd tried once upon a time with his parents, but that had never worked.

'I'll be very careful,' he said. 'I don't want any more scars.'

She lay on fragrant moss under the dense trees of a forest. The leaves above her moved with a sound like gentle breath, giving her glimpses of hidden stars. All around her, quiet life: sap in trunks, water in grass, fireflies blinking their way.

This was what her parents had fought for. All life one life, all earth together, united in love. This was what she had read about, seeing the images in her head with the clarity of a dream.

Something like a breeze feathered over her body, stirred her skin into life. She closed her eyes in pleasure, opened her eyes again into daylight, and was awake.

Angus lay behind her in his bed, his body curled into hers. She could feel his breath on the back of her ear and his hand feathering over her skin. Leisurely, so lightly that he felt like the breeze she'd dreamed about, his right hand travelled over her belly, up to hold her breast, tease her nipple. Then to the other breast, and then down the line of her waist and hip, between her legs.

A lazy Sunday morning making love. She made a little cosy sound to let him know she was awake, and nestled further back into him. The lean length of his body surrounded her; a slight shift, and he was sliding inside her. He'd been awake, she thought with a sleepy smile, he'd planned to wake her up like this.

He nuzzled her hair aside and kissed the back of her neck as he moved deeper inside her. 'Good morning, beautiful,' he whispered. She pushed her bottom back, took the entire length of him in, and he held her there for a moment.

She felt full, content, whole, excited. Kept safe in the circle of Angus's arms, his strong body behind her, the two of them joined. As she'd felt held by the forest in her dream.

He found her clitoris with his fingers and stroked her gently, to a slow rhythm that he soon matched with his body. Exquisite caresses, inside and out. She reached behind her and touched his lean hip, his hair-roughened thigh. Because she couldn't see him her fingertips seemed doubly sensitive.

'You are the most wonderful feeling I've ever had,' Angus murmured in her ear.

He'd awakened her in so many ways. She arched into him, tightened her muscles around him, tried to get him still deeper. He was slow and gentle and tender. Elisabeth closed her eyes and imagined him in her dream forest with her. Weaving his magic with his body.

Behind her closed eyes everything was green, vibrant, alive. She felt his breath on the skin beneath her ear and her nipples tightened, her skin tingled. Her body reached for its climax in slow, maddening steps.

And she could feel Angus getting closer, although his movements stayed unhurried. She'd learned him after all these times making love. His breathing was faster, his thigh hot and hard beneath her hand, tensing with every slow thrust. She pictured his face as she'd seen it before, teeth clenched, eyes narrow and dark as he fought to keep control of the overwhelming pleasure. Waiting for her, trying to give her the best he could, relishing every second of the build-up and anticipation.

But it had built. She was nearly there. She tightened her hand on his thigh and squeezed his penis hard inside her. 'Come with me,' she said, and heard him take a great shuddery breath and then let it out as a cry as he thrust hard, once, pulsed and she pressed back against him, thrashing her head in her own orgasm.

He held her close as their breathing slowed, and then she twisted her head back and kissed him. When she opened her eyes she saw his grey ones looking back at her, steady and intense and with something in them she didn't quite understand.

He'd been looking at her like that a lot this weekend. As if he were searching her. Assessing her.

Elisabeth turned back around. Nestled in his embrace, she should feel safe, as she had a moment before. But she didn't, not quite.

'What time is it?' she asked.

'About eight.'

'Do you have to work today?'

'Magnum for ten.' His voice sounded sleepy and sated.

'It's my turn to make you Sunday breakfast in bed.'

He grunted, and she could hear he was smiling. 'Don't burn it.'

She sat up and swatted him on his bare shoulder. 'It's not my fault I'm an appalling cook. Blame my teacher.'

'I'll find him and shoot him after breakfast.' He caught her wrist and pulled her down with him for another kiss. Angus was warm with sleep and lovemaking. She relaxed into him for a blissful minute, and then got up.

'Thanks, love,' he mumbled into the pillow.

She looked at him as she pulled on the jeans and shirt Angus had taken off her last night. His eyes were closed and the dark lashes fanned his cheeks. The skin of his eyelids was soft-looking, vulnerable. His hair was tousled, his cheeks touched with pink. His left hand, curled by his chin, had a blue catering plaster around its injured thumb.

Despite the breadth of his shoulders, the muscles of his arms, the hair scattered across his chest, he looked like a young boy. Innocent and contented. She smiled and went down the stairs and into the kitchen.

Confronted with Angus's kitchen, she doubted her ability to cook breakfast. Everything was stainless steel and spotless granite. The utensils that hung from the walls resembled instruments of torture. There were so many cupboards and drawers that it would probably take her hours to find what she wanted. Whatever that might be.

Flicking through the TV channels one night she'd seen one of his cooking shows from his last series. It had been filmed in this room. Angus had whipped up something amazing in no time whatsoever and made it look incredibly easy. Whereas she thought that, in this kitchen, she would be doing well if she could manage to boil water without breaking something.

With the thought, she smiled. Angus's favourite food: boiled eggs and toast soldiers. That, she could handle.

She unlocked the back door and went out to the back garden to the chicken coop, which was tucked away in the back corner of the garden. He'd told her he bribed the neighbours with fresh eggs and baked goods made with them so they wouldn't mind the noise of his two chickens. Apparently he was out here at all hours after work mucking out so there wouldn't be an odour.

Keeping chickens in London. It was completely impractical, especially for a man who worked every hour God sent.

She said hello to MacNugget and Kiev in their run, unlocked the door to the coop, and found two eggs warm in the nest. On the way back to the kitchen she thought of Angus warm in his bed.

And suddenly she understood why he went to all the trouble of keeping the chickens.

*Food is emotion,* he'd told her. Danny and Jennifer loved foods that reminded them of times before their troubles had begun; Elisabeth remembered what she was eating when she'd discovered her favourite escape. Angus's favourite meal was the only one he could remember having been cooked for him growing up.

Angus MacAllister kept an egg factory in his back garden just so he'd never go without the comfort he'd felt, briefly, all those years ago.

The thought made her want to run upstairs and kiss him. But if food was emotion, boiled eggs and toast soldiers would show how she felt about him much more than kisses would.

She put the eggs carefully on the counter and searched for several minutes until she found a small pan. She glimpsed a strange assortment of appliances in the cupboards, but nothing overtly resembling a toaster. Considering he went to all the trouble of keeping chickens, odds were he had a toaster, too, but she decided not to waste her time looking for it when the grill would do for toast. She filled the pan with water, put the eggs in, located the timer on the cooker, and starting hunting for bread and butter.

Ten minutes later, she opened the freezer in desperation and found about a million ice-cube trays and three containers of chocolate ice cream. No sliced white bread, the staple of most households the length and breadth of Britain.

'Shop,' she said to herself. Fortunately it was easy to find her shoes and handbag, abandoned by the front door last night, and Angus's keys in the bowl in the hallway. She stepped outside.

Elisabeth wasn't sure what direction a shop was in, but, figuring in central London any direction would lead her to one eventually, she locked Angus's door behind her and turned left up the street.

The weather was bright and sunny. There was a gentle breeze that ruffled her hair as she walked. The plane trees that lined the street rustled their leaves like the trees in her dream this morning.

Dreams, poetry, novels: they all had hidden meanings, messages you could puzzle out if you chose. She'd found that idea endlessly fascinating at school, as if there were a secret code in a book waiting for her to discover it. She thought of her dream this morning of being in a night forest, held close, and how it had turned out to be Angus touching her, making morning love.

Why a forest? she wondered idly, swinging the ring of keys from her fingers, enjoying the chiming sound they made. It wasn't a memory; she'd spent plenty of time in Canadian forests, but this hadn't been like that. It had been quiet, supernaturally green, friendlier than the wilderness of Saskatchewan. An enchanted place.

Like the setting of the play she was teaching at school.

She stopped the keys swinging, silenced their music. That was what she'd dreamed. Shakespeare's magical forest in *A Midsummer Night's Dream,* where mortals were tricked into falling in love.

And she'd dreamed it because that was happening to her.

Despite all her worries, all her promises to herself to keep herself safe. She was falling in love with Angus.

The way she felt cherished. How she wanted to spend every moment with him. Even this symbolic, emotional breakfast she was about to cook for him.

She was falling in love with him and she should have recognised the signs from her time with Robin, from all the books she'd read, should have recognised and stepped back before she lost so much control that she could only understand what was going on when she was told by her dreams.

She'd reached a corner shop; caught up in her thoughts, she pushed on the door. When it didn't budge she focused her eyes and saw there was a young woman on the other side of the glass. 'Pull,' mouthed the woman, smiling. Elisabeth pulled the door open and stood aside to let the woman past.

She held the hand of a little blond boy, a toddler. He had his arm clasped around a plastic bottle of milk, his face screwed up with the concentration required not to drop it.

'Thanks,' said the woman, picked up her son, and walked down the street with him in her arms. Elisabeth watched them go.

*Mine would have been that age now,* she thought.

Two years on, it hurt less. It had to. But she still marked it with children she saw, charted the growth that wouldn't happen.

Angus had said he wouldn't do what Robin had done. But Robin had been the least of what she had lost. She'd lost her baby, lost her hopes, lost a part of herself she'd never seen again.

And here she was jumping right back into love.

The woman and the child rounded the corner out of sight. Elisabeth went into the shop and found a plastic-wrapped loaf of bread on the dim shelves and a cube of butter in the chill cabinet in the back. She waited at the till behind an elderly man who was laboriously unloading a basketful of cat-food tins onto the counter.

Her gaze wandered around the shop without taking anything in, finally settling on the piles of newspapers by the counter. Automatically, her arm stretched out to pick up the thick paper she normally read on a Sunday, stacked beside the tabloids.

She stopped. Her fingers loosened on the bread and it dropped to the floor with a plastic thump.

CHEF GOES BACK TO SCHOOL! screamed the headline. It was under the red banner of one of the nation's most popular tabloid newspapers.

And it was over a photograph of Angus MacAllister and Elisabeth. And another photograph of Angus and Jennifer and Danny, outside Chanticleer.

Elisabeth was very good with dealing with crises. After all, she had been a teacher for quite a few years now. She put down the butter on the counter, and retrieved the bread from the floor and put it on a nearby shelf. Then she picked up the tabloid and began reading.

TV chef ANGUS MACALLISTER has been donating his time to help TWO SCHOOLCHILDREN learn how to cook for a prestigious competition. And the chef has helped himself to a side dish, too—he's been GETTING SAUCY with sexy teacher ELISABETH READ.

Enough. Elisabeth paid for the paper and folded it in half so she wouldn't have to see any more. She walked back to Angus's house, her mouth a firm line, her hands clenched.

Here was what she got for falling in love. A hard kick in the teeth.

She saw the man with the camera outside Angus's house, and wondered whether he'd been there when she'd left, when she'd been too enchanted by her silly dream to see him. She held the newspaper in front of her face to hide it from the lens, unlocked Angus's door and went straight up to his bedroom. When she entered, he raised his head from the pillow and smiled at her.

'Don't tell me you've made breakfast already.' He sniffed the air. 'I don't smell any burning.'

'It's all a joke to you, isn't it, Angus? Aren't you funny? Aren't you clever? Aren't you *famous?*'

He sat up abruptly at her tone, the sheets pooling around his waist. 'Elisabeth? What's wrong?'

'What's wrong is that I trusted you. Against my better judgement, as you know, because you told me you really cared, that this wasn't all a publicity stunt.' She laughed without humour. 'Imagine my surprise down at the newsagent's. Were you going to tell me or were you hoping I wouldn't notice?'

'Notice what?' He pulled the sheets aside and sat on the side of the bed, and he was so naked, so beautiful, so looking at her with that intentness and false innocence that she felt her anger rising up in her even stronger.

The meetings with his publicist. The phone calls, the luring the kids away from school to some place where the paparazzi could photograph them. Every single thing the two of them had done together.

'This,' she snapped, and thrust the newspaper at him. He took it and spread it open on his bare knee.

'Oh, bugger,' he said.

'Didn't catch your best side?'

'Christine's bloody leaks to the press,' he muttered, and stood up. 'Listen, I didn't mean for this to happen—'

'You didn't mean for me to see it, you mean. Do you really expect me to believe that you gave up a chance for publicity because of the kids? Or me? I mean, come on, Angus. You thought this whole thing up for publicity. What am I? Sex? Whereas if you're famous, you have the whole world on your side.'

'Elisabeth.' He reached for her. 'I swear to you, this is a mistake.'

She stepped back from him. 'The only mistake you've made is if you think I'm going to let you touch me any more. Goodbye, Angus.'

She turned on her heel and stormed down the stairs, not listening to his voice behind her calling her name, his footsteps on the carpet. He caught up with her as she was turning the doorknob and put himself between her and the door.

'Sweetheart, I know what you're thinking, but it isn't true. I had nothing to do with this.'

She gritted her teeth at the endearment. He thought charm and the sight of his nude body were still going to work.

'Get out of my way,' she said.

He crossed his arms on his chest, and she saw his eyes flare with anger. 'You wouldn't treat one of your students like this, would you? What about if this were Danny, not me? Would you assume he was guilty without hearing his side of the story?'

Her hand was on the doorknob. She turned it and started to push open the door.

'I suggest you step away from the door unless you want to get photographed naked,' she said, and ducked around him and out of the house.

She held her handbag up in front of her face to shield herself from the lens, hurried down the street, and got into the first cab she could hail.

# CHAPTER TWELVE

ANGUS put down the phone and swore.

Well, the media leak wasn't Christine's fault; she'd said she'd stopped contact with the press as soon as he'd asked her last week, and he believed her. Besides the fact that she'd always been trustworthy, he was paying her enough so that she should follow his wishes even if she disapproved of them.

Which meant that the tabloid had picked up the story on its own.

And which meant that he'd lost Elisabeth without doing anything wrong.

He went back up to his bedroom to put on some clothes and saw the bed where he'd made love with Elisabeth not an hour ago. The print of her body was still on the sheets and pillow— he could see the indentations of hip, shoulder, cheek.

He tugged the sheets straight and lifted the pillow to shake it back into shape. She'd jumped to conclusions, accused him without any evidence. As he'd said, she wouldn't treat her students that way. But with Angus, the man she'd laughed with, worked with, made love with, she'd assumed he was guilty.

She cared less about him than she cared about kids she was paid to look after.

He pulled on some clothes, picked up the newspaper he'd dropped on the floor, and went back downstairs. In the kitchen, Angus got out a spoon, opened the freezer, and took out a carton of chocolate ice cream.

Cold, creamy, melting, heavenly. The breakfast of champions, and one of the only one-hundred-per-cent guaranteed methods to make yourself feel better.

It tasted of dust.

As he set the ice cream and the paper down on the table he spotted the pan on the hob. He walked over to it and looked inside.

He stared at the eggs and the water for a long time.

This was the breakfast she'd been about to make him.

He remembered the way Elisabeth had looked when she'd left: her cheeks and lips ash-white, her eyes wide. She'd spat out her words, enunciating each one too clearly. She'd looked furious.

And absolutely terrified.

He'd seen her defences when the condom had split. What if she'd accused him not because she didn't care, but because she did?

She'd jumped to a conclusion, but that conclusion wasn't too far-fetched, considering the person he'd tried his best to be for the past fourteen years.

Not long ago, he would have let Christine leak the information to the press. The reason he hadn't was because falling in love with Elisabeth had changed him. But she didn't know that he was in love with her. Therefore, she couldn't know how he had changed.

Therefore, he had to tell her. He had to show her.

He picked up the kitchen extension and called Elisabeth's mobile number. It went straight to voicemail.

*Elisabeth, I love you,* he thought, but he wasn't going to take the biggest risk he'd ever taken in his life to an answerphone.

'It's me,' he said instead. 'We need to talk. I don't know how the paper got hold of the story, but I'm going to find out. Give me a ring back. Please.'

He tried her home number too, but that was answered by the machine. He left a similar message there. He'd give her half an hour to get home and hear his messages and then he'd go to her flat.

Then, he'd knock down her door if he had to, and he'd stand in front of her and say, 'I love you.' Those three words, just like that. And somehow he'd find a way to say them so that she wouldn't doubt his sincerity, so she would be willing to listen, so she would smile at him and kiss him and say, 'I love you too.'

Somehow.

Meanwhile, he'd figure out how the tabloid had got hold of this story. He called Henry to say he'd be late and to warn him that Magnum might get some reporters, and then he took his carton and spoon to the table and opened up the newspaper. The photograph of him and Elisabeth had been taken during their walk through Kensington Gardens. Elisabeth was smiling; Angus was leaning towards her to steal a kiss. They were holding hands. The paparazzi must have followed them all last weekend without their noticing.

He read down the article, wincing at the poor cooking puns, and then his eyes widened. He put his spoonful of ice cream back into the carton untouched.

Mystery solved. He knew how the newspaper had found out at least some of the story.

He left the ice cream on the table and headed for the door.

As soon as the taxi pulled up in front of her house she saw the two men standing outside, one with a camera. She leaned forward to speak to the driver. 'Actually, I think I'd like to go to the Victoria and Albert Museum, please.'

She spent the day in the museum, walking along with the crowds looking at the Raphael cartoons, wandering the empty high-ceilinged cast rooms on her own, feeling safely anonymous. The order and the history should have soothed her. But it didn't.

Once again, she'd fallen in love with a man who'd betrayed her—or, just as bad, who'd let his paid minions do it for him. She might have a degree from Cambridge, but she was the stupidest person she knew.

After the museum closed she got the underground back to her part of town and walked the half a mile or so to Joanna's flat. If Joanna would let her stay the night and borrow some clothes for school tomorrow, she wouldn't have to face anybody from the press.

When she rounded the corner of Joanna's street, though, she saw the door to her basement flat open and Joanna emerge up the stairs with a tall, dark, slender man. Elisabeth stopped walking and watched her friend and the man pause at pavement level and share a long, passionate kiss.

Elisabeth turned around and headed back to her own flat. Joanna had her own love life to deal with; she didn't need to help Elisabeth out with her disasters.

Cautiously she approached her own building. First, she scanned for Angus's car and frowned at herself when she was disappointed not to see it. Surely if he were innocent, he'd be trying to find her to explain?

She looked around for the reporters she'd seen that morning. The coast looked clear. But she couldn't be sure.

She dug a pair of sunglasses out of her bag and put them on, let her hair fall around her face, and ran for it.

'I feel like a freaking secret agent,' she muttered as she unlocked her door as fast as she could and slammed it behind her, then sprinted up the stairs to her flat and slammed that door behind her too.

Her bell began ringing as soon as she'd caught her breath. The red light on her answerphone was blinking frantically.

She unplugged it and the phone as well. She examined her doorbell but couldn't figure out how to disable it. She hung a towel over it instead, turned on some loud music, and went to fill herself a bath.

Sleep eluded her. She was relieved when the clock said six-thirty and she could stop pretending to try to read her book and start getting ready for school. If she got there early, she could prepare all her lessons down to the minute, covering every eventuality. It could be a day without surprises.

There wasn't anybody outside her flat—even predators had to sleep, she guessed—but she kept her hat on anyway as she walked to school and went in the back entrance by the kitchen. If she was lucky the tabloids had got the message that she didn't want to talk and wouldn't bother to come to her school.

She doubted it, though.

She was writing instructions on the board for her first lesson when the door of her classroom opened and Jo came in. She looked pale and worried.

'Here you are,' she said. 'I've been trying to get in touch with you since last night.'

'I turned off my phones,' Elisabeth said.

'I know.' Jo came to her and hugged her. 'I've been worried about you, love.'

Elisabeth swallowed hard. 'I'm okay.'

Jo pulled back and studied her face. 'No, you're not. You're in a state and I can't blame you. You look like you haven't slept a wink and, knowing you, you haven't eaten a thing for hours and hours.'

Food? That was the furthest thing from her mind. 'No. But I'm fine.'

'Bull. Here, have this. And you'd better eat it; I'm going to watch you.' She produced one of her chocolate bars from a pocket and handed it to Elisabeth. Knowing she didn't have a choice, Elisabeth sat down, unwrapped it and took a bite.

'Chocolate isn't a healthy breakfast,' Elisabeth said.

'It's better than nothing. Listen, I hate to say this, but Howard wants to talk to you about the newspaper thing.'

She should have known that the head teacher would have something to say about the kids being featured in the national press. 'Of course. I should've rung him yesterday, but I was distracted. Thanks, Jo.' She rose.

'Hold on, you're not going anywhere without this.' Jo picked up the chocolate bar she'd left on the desk. 'And I'll walk with you to make sure you eat it.'

Elisabeth bit into the chocolate obediently as they walked the short distance down the hall to the head's office. 'So how's Angus taking the media intrusion?' Jo asked.

'Angus thrives on media intrusion,' Elisabeth said. 'I'm sure he's doing fine.'

'And when are you going to tell me all about your saucy nights together?'

Elisabeth made a face. 'It is so unappealing to have your private life made the subject of bad writing.'

'I don't care how it's written about, I just want to know one thing: are you in love with him?'

The chocolate turned to a lump in her mouth. She swallowed it with difficulty. Jo's words had been said in her usual lively, flippant tone but her friend was looking at her seriously.

'Yes, I am,' she answered. 'But—'

Jo interrupted her by flinging her arms around her. 'Oh, Elisabeth, that's wonderful. I'm so, so pleased. You deserve happiness and he's exactly the person to give it to you.'

'He's not giving me anything,' Elisabeth said grimly. 'He—'

They'd reached the head's office, which opened immediately. Obviously Howard had been waiting for them to come and had heard the sound of their voices.

'Elisabeth,' he said, and, though Elisabeth hadn't been nervous about speaking to him before, her stomach suddenly twisted at something in his tone. He was a fairly easygoing man on day-to-day matters, but he had very definite views about how his school would be run.

'Thanks for meeting with me,' he said. 'Please, come in and sit down.'

Jo gave her a surreptitious squeeze on the shoulder before Elisabeth went into Howard's office and shut the door behind her.

The office was painted a light blue. Elisabeth supposed it was meant to be soothing. However, the sight of the red-topped tabloid on Howard's desk pretty much negated the effects of the paint.

'I'm sorry I didn't call you earlier,' she said, sitting in one of the blue chairs across from Howard's desk. 'I'd unplugged my phone.'

'I did try calling you, but we need to talk face to face anyway.' He sat in his own chair and toyed with the edge of the newspaper. 'I was very surprised to see this story. I thought we had agreed about the level of media exposure.'

'I know, and, believe me, I'm as upset about seeing Jennifer and Danny in the newspaper as you are.'

'Your personal life, of course, is your own. And you know that you're a valued teacher at this school. But I've already had several telephone calls from parents, not to mention the journalists ringing for comments. Jennifer's father is unhappy about the story, and Daniel's parents are understandably worried about how the attention will affect their son. Especially when their names are linked with a story about their teacher's love life.'

Elisabeth gnawed her lip. 'I feel horrible about it, Howard. If it helps, I can assure you that I won't be seeing Mr MacAllister in a private capacity any more.'

'As I said, Elisabeth, your private life is your own. I have nothing to say about that, insofar as it doesn't impact the school.'

Howard was a nice man, Elisabeth thought. She could name other head teachers who would be hitting her with both barrels right now. 'Thanks, Howard.'

'However, I can't let this grow any further. Angus MacAllister's involvement with the school was on the condition that the children wouldn't be identified. Given what's happened, I think it's best that he stop his lessons with the students.'

'But—what about Jennifer and Danny?'

'They can still compete. I've heard that they've made great progress. They're a credit to the school. Tasha Cutter can take over helping them.'

Howard was not a nice man. How could he snatch away Jennifer and Danny's chances like this?

'They've made great progress, but that's entirely due to Angus. You know what they were like before. And their last re-hearsal was a disaster. Without him, they're in danger of losing their confidence. And the competition is Saturday.'

'I'm sorry, Elisabeth. We can't afford to risk the school's reputation or distract the other students. And, in any case, our agreement with Mr MacAllister has been broken.'

Pale with anger, she rose from her chair. 'If that's your final decision, I'll have to accept it. But I hope you'll reconsider.'

'It's my final decision. And please sit down; we need to talk about something else.'

She frowned, but sat. 'Yes, Howard?'

'I was hoping you could explain to me why you gave the paper an interview.'

'What?'

'I must say, I was surprised. You've always had excellent pro-fessional judgement. Why did you agree to speak to a journalist?'

She stared at Howard, who appeared to be serious. 'I didn't speak to any journalists. I've been avoiding them.'

'Then how did they get these quotes?' He held out the newspaper to her, and she seized it.

Same headline. Same photographs. She hadn't read any further than the first paragraph yesterday. She skimmed down the article and then felt her mouth dropping open.

In an exclusive interview, Elisabeth Read told this paper that Angus, once voted the fifth sexiest man in Britain, had 'swept her off her feet'. Though MacAllister has been linked with a bevy of beauties in the past, Elisabeth seems to be playing for keeps.

'It's early to be thinking marriage,' she said, 'but I want children eventually.'

And the celebrity chef seems to be getting straight A's with the stunning teacher, who took a FIRST-CLASS degree in English literature from CAMBRIDGE UNIVERSITY.

'He's very talented,' the statuesque brunette told us with a smile.

'Oh,' she said.

Howard was clearly waiting for her to say something more. She searched through the rest of the article, which went on in a similarly puerile vein, but didn't find any more quotes.

Where had they got them? They seemed a little familiar. She looked at the byline: Clive Jones.

The Welsh tango-dancer. He hadn't been after a date.

She folded the paper in half, and sighed deeply.

'I think I have made a very stupid mistake,' she said.

'Are you saying you didn't mean to give that interview?'

'I thought I was having a private conversation.'

Howard nodded. 'I see. Well, that makes this easier. Let me say, Elisabeth, that you are an excellent teacher, and your career at this school is not under review at this time.'

She hadn't thought her stomach could sink any lower. But it did.

'That statement sounds like it's about to have a "but" after it.'

'Yes. But you're the focus of media attention, whether or not you meant to give that interview. I don't know how long this story will run, but right now there are reporters outside the school. Jennifer and Daniel are minors, and we can take steps to protect them from public exposure. You are not. It's June, Elisabeth. You'll understand we can't have anything happen to distract the students who are sitting their public exams.'

She saw what was coming. 'Oh, please, no, Howard.'

'I've spoken with the governors and it's best that you take some time away from school. Until this all calms down.'

'I see,' she said, numb. 'Is that all?'

'Yes.' She had to give him credit; Howard's face was sympathetic. 'I've arranged to cover your classes for this week, and then we'll review the situation on Friday. Joanna Graham will take over your tutor group.'

So Jo had known. No wonder she'd been so worried. Elisabeth stood. 'I'd better go and sort out the work for my classes.'

Howard also stood. 'I hope everything will be back to normal very soon. And of course, even if you're not here, you should go to the Kid Culinaire competition on Saturday if you like. You've worked hard to make sure those students do well.'

And she'd also done the one thing to ensure that they would fail. She nodded, and went out of the head's office.

Jo was waiting for her in the corridor. 'Elisabeth, I'm sorry. I tried to talk him out of it.'

Elisabeth shook her head. 'I've been so stupid.'

'I told Howard there was no way you gave that interview intentionally. How did they trick you into it? Did they call you out of the blue or something?'

'It was Clive. Did you know he was a reporter?'

'Who's Clive?'

'The Welsh tango dancer you tried to set me up with?'

Jo blushed. She had known he was a reporter, Elisabeth thought, feeling another twinge of betrayal.

'The tango dancer's called Dewi Thomas,' Jo said. 'I—I thought, since you were getting closer to Angus, you wouldn't be interested in him. So I gave him a whirl myself this weekend.'

'Dewi—he's not called Clive?'

Elisabeth leaned against the wall of the corridor, feeling like the biggest fool in the universe.

'The reporter was Welsh,' she said. 'I only talked to him because I thought you were trying to set us up.'

Jo looked stricken. 'Oh, God, Liz, I'm sorry.'

'It's not your fault. It's mine. I'm a total idiot.'

'You're not an idiot. You're in love. You're allowed to be ditzy.'

Elisabeth wiped her hand over her face. 'I accused Angus of leaking the story to the press. And it was me who gave the interview all along. I hate to differ with you, but I am an idiot.'

The bell rang and the corridor started to be filled with students in their maroon uniforms. Groups of them stared at Elisabeth as they walked by. 'Hey, miss, I saw you in the paper!' one of them shouted.

'Duck into the staff room,' Jo recommended. 'I've got to go. I'll call you later.' She gave Elisabeth a quick hug and disappeared through the crowds.

Elisabeth knew how to fake a dignity she didn't possess. She raised her chin and as she walked to the staff room she greeted each student who met her eye by name, and greeted every comment about the papers with a cheerful, 'Good morning.'

Very quickly, she stopped hearing comments. Of course, that meant they were talking twice as hard behind her back.

By the time she got to the staff room she was exhausted. It was emptying out as the teachers headed for their form rooms for registration; still, she noticed, the news had spread. Her colleagues were less obvious about scoping her out than the students had been, but only barely.

Her sole consolation was that she knew Howard was professional enough not to have mentioned her suspension to anybody but senior members of staff directly involved, like Jo, before he told her himself. So she had enough time to get out of school before the rumours started to spread in earnest.

Before that, she had to plan work for her lessons for a week. And before that, she had a phone call to make.

She waited until the last teacher had left the room until she took her phone from her bag and turned it on for the first time since yesterday morning. It started beeping immediately with missed call and message alerts.

She ignored them, and dialled Angus's number.

It was before lunch. The interior of Magnum was all white, clean lines, punctuated by bright flowers on the tables and abstract art on the walls. The entire centre of the room was taken up by a floor-to-ceiling round aquarium, which bathed the white room in a soft liquid glow. The fish inside it were live echoes of the flowers.

An architectural representation of Angus MacAllister: attention-grabbing, beautiful, with something alive and wonderful at the centre. Elisabeth touched a petal of a fuchsia gerbera in the vase next to her and went through what she'd planned to say. She'd had enough of the unexpected to last a very long time.

The door to the kitchen opened and Angus came out, dressed in chef whites that emphasised the darkness of his hair, the breadth of his shoulders.

She drew in a quick breath. The one thing she hadn't been able to plan was how he reacted to seeing her. She'd run through all the possibilities on the tube over here: anger, bitterness, reproach, disappointment, indifference.

Instead, he was smiling.

'Elisabeth,' he said and his voice was so warm and throaty she wanted to curl up inside it and rest. He came towards her across the breadth of the empty dining room.

She hadn't known what his response would be, but she'd known what hers would be. So she followed her plan and clasped her hands together so she couldn't reach for him.

'I'm sorry, Angus,' she said. 'I jumped to conclusions and accused you of something of which you were innocent without hearing your side of the story. Moreover, the source of the fault was actually myself. It was an unconscionable action and I apologise.'

He'd stopped walking when she'd started speaking, and now he leaned his shoulder against the side of the aquarium, his smile widening. 'How many times did you rehearse that? You sound just like a textbook.'

'A few times. But it's still sincere.'

'I know.' He came a little closer. 'You didn't know he was a reporter, did you?'

'No.'

'You have to watch out for that in this business. One time in the early days I played darts with a bloke in a pub and read my conversation word-for-word the next morning.'

'Well, I'm not in your business and I don't ever intend to be, but it was a silly thing to do no matter what. And I shouldn't have said those things to you.'

He shrugged. 'Maybe not. But I haven't exactly been backward with publicity for the past few years. It was understandable.'

'You're acting as if you don't mind, but you must be angry.'

'I was. I'm not any more.' He closed the distance between them, and touched her chin with his fingers, tilted her head up to look her in the eyes. 'I'm so glad to see you. I spent most of yesterday ringing your doorbell.'

She stepped back and it hurt much more than she'd expected it to. 'I need your help, Angus.'

He narrowed his eyes. 'What's wrong?'

'Has the school called you yet?'

'No.' He pulled out a chair for her at the table they were closest to, and waited until she sat before he did.

'They want you to stop working with Jennifer and Danny.'

Angus sucked in a long breath, and then let it out. 'Well, I suppose they're nearly ready. If they can do some more practice—'

'It's not just practice they need. They need stability and a routine. If we change everything now, Jennifer will lose confidence, and who knows what Danny will decide to do? They have to practise with you.'

'But if the school doesn't want me—'

'Then we need to find someplace else they can work.'

She saw Angus thinking, and she bit her lip, realising that she loved him just as much when they were working together as when they were in bed together.

'They can come here,' he said. 'I'll cancel my early bookings for the next few nights. They'll be in a professional kitchen. Once they get used to it, that will help.'

She nodded. 'Thank you. I'll ring their parents to try to get permission.'

'As long as you're here with them, I don't see how that will be a problem.'

She shifted in her chair. 'I wish I were as certain as you are. Their parents might not be so keen on the idea when they find out I've been suspended from school.'

Angus stared. 'You've been suspended from school?'

'Just for a week. Until things calm down.' She laughed, though she felt far from confident. 'It gives me time to catch up on my reading, anyway.'

'Damn, Elisabeth. That's not right.'

'I understand the head's reasons. He's putting the students first, and that's right, no matter what.'

'And you're putting them first, too. How do *you* feel about this?'

She saw the gerberas blur before her eyes. 'Terrible. The entire school is talking about me behind my back. My classes are being taken care of by other people. I'm a story instead of a person.' She swallowed. 'I feel as if I'm holding on by my fingernails.'

Angus got out of his chair, took her hand, and raised her to stand close to him. He wrapped his arms around her.

'The important thing,' he said, kissing her forehead with warm, wonderful lips, 'is that we're together again. I have to tell you something.'

His embrace, his kisses were a siren song she had already steeled herself against. She held his wrists and disengaged herself from him, stepped back from his body.

Even though every inch of her was screaming at her not to do it, every inch of her had been very wrong before.

'We can't be together again, Angus,' she said. 'It's not your fault, but my feelings make me do stupid things when I'm around you. I've messed up Jennifer and Danny's chances. My job is at risk. And you—' she had to look away from his grey eyes '—I hurt you too. It has to stop.'

'All those things will be all right. The kids will be fine; you'll be back in school in no time. And I'm pretty tough.' She felt his hands on her shoulders, drawing her close again.

'No.' She pulled away. 'It's not just those things. It's everything. Since the moment I met you I've been loose, I've been out of control, I've been spinning. I'm exhausted just trying to keep myself together.'

'You don't have to keep yourself together, Elisabeth,' he said quietly. 'I'm safe. You can trust me.'

'You're not safe,' she said. 'Because if I can't keep myself together I don't know who I am. I can't do it, Angus.'

'Try.'

Throaty, raspy, precious. She looked at his scarred hands, hanging loose by his sides. Thought of everything they could do.

'I can't,' she said. 'I need to live on an even keel; I need to understand what's happening around me. All of this is—' she gestured '—too much. You're too intense, Angus, your world is too wide open to everyone and everything. I can't cope with it any more.'

He didn't say anything. She looked at his face. It was still and unsmiling. His eyes looked dulled.

God, she wanted to hold him.

She drew herself upright. 'I think you're an incredible person. And you're a very good man. I loved being with you, and I have an enormous amount of respect for you.' He flinched ever so slightly at the word.

She hurried on, knowing her words were inadequate, knowing they weren't telling the real truth. But if she said the real truth, she'd throw away everything and get back together with Angus. And she couldn't.

'It was fun,' she said, 'but now it's over.'

'It was fun,' he echoed. He sank into his chair, his shoulders slumped. 'I'm going to need to buy some more ice cream.'

She thought about asking what he meant, but that would draw her into more conversation, and the more time she spent with him, the more she wanted to forget about everything she had just said. She pushed her chair back under the table.

'I'll go and get in touch with Jennifer and Danny's parents, then,' she said. 'When should I say you'll have them here?'

'Tomorrow at five.' He was staring at the table top, and she got the impression he wasn't really thinking about what he was saying. 'That should be fine. Better make it Thursday and Friday, too.'

Three nights of restaurant business cancelled to help a couple of schoolchildren. 'Thank you, Angus. You really are extraordinary.'

He nodded, and then suddenly looked into her face. 'You'll be here too, of course.'

'I—'

'You said yourself that they need stability and a routine.'

'I did.' That would be three more rehearsals with Angus, and then the competition on Saturday. Hours and hours with him. Probably too much, but nowhere near enough.

'All right,' she said. She leaned forward and pressed a swift kiss on his cheek. 'I'll see you tomorrow,' she said, and left the restaurant before she could kiss him any more, satisfy her mouth and hands and heart. Before she lost control again.

Because if she lost it again, she wasn't sure she would ever get it back.

# CHAPTER THIRTEEN

LONDON never really got dark.

Streetlamps, passing cars, the light peeping out through house curtains. Traffic lights changing from red to yellow to green, telling empty streets to go.

London at night was amber and grey and blue. Not black, but different enough from the day to give a feeling of anonymity. Out here at night, Angus MacAllister was another shape. Nobody special.

As he walked he felt the throb of thousands of people around him. Breathed in the smoke of a cigarette or the smell of cooking, even at this hour. He loved London; in London you were never alone.

And he needed reminding of that because, right now, Angus felt more alone than he ever had in his life, even during that Easter holiday when he had been very small in his parents' big house in Scotland.

It was Friday night. No, it was Saturday morning.

And after Saturday afternoon, he would probably have no reason ever to see Elisabeth Read again.

He shoved his hands into his pockets and kept walking. He wasn't going to sleep, anyway. And sleep without Elisabeth beside him was restless, nearly as exhausting as being awake.

*I love you.* He'd been all ready to say it to her. For the first time in his life, to lay his heart in all honesty before someone. Not to impress, not to charm. To offer.

And she'd stepped away and said it was over before it had even begun.

The Royal Albert Hall was lit up like a blood-red wedding cake. Kensington Gardens were cool and dark and he'd walked there with Elisabeth. He turned right, into the quiet streets of South Kensington.

He hadn't been able to say it to her. Why say it when he was going to be rejected? There was no point.

All the times he'd wanted to call his parents, for example. When he'd earned his first Michelin star. *See, I can do it. There's nothing wrong with me. Even you have to be impressed by this.*

He'd had a party instead.

Angus kicked at a lamppost. Even if he'd wanted to in the past week, Elisabeth hadn't given him the chance to tell her he loved her. She'd turned up to Magnum at the same time as the kids, and focused all her attention on them. Everything he'd said had been met with coolness. She'd refused to see him alone. It was like when he'd first met her. Except hugely different, because now it hurt.

His mobile phone rang and vibrated in his jacket pocket. He took it out; the screen glowed. He didn't recognise the number, which was another mobile. Not Elisabeth. With a detached interest he noticed the time: two twenty-six.

'Hello?' he said into it. Distraction was good. Even though the news at this time of night was bound to be bad.

'Angus?'

He stopped walking. The voice was very small and very quiet, though there was a lot of background noise.

'Danny?' he said. 'Where are you?'

'In the back of a car.'

'What's wrong?'

'I think I'm about to get nicked.'

Angus swore. 'Where are you?'

After a pause, Danny gave him a location south of the Thames. 'And you stole the car?' Angus asked.

'My mates. I don't know what to do. Mum and Dad will kill me—'

'And why do you think you're about to get nicked?'

'Because the police just stopped us.' He was whispering now.

'Okay. I'll be there as soon as I can. Danny, you've been bloody stupid, do you know that? The competition is tomorrow. Today.'

'I—they wanted to and I couldn't say anything, because—'

Exactly. 'I'll be there. Don't do anything else foolish.'

He ended the call and while he was looking for a cab in the empty streets he dialled another number with his thumb by feel. When he raised the phone to his ear it was ringing.

And ringing. Voicemail answered; he hung up and tried again. A third time.

'Hello?' Elisabeth's voice was bleary with sleep. He pictured her with rumpled hair and flushed cheeks, her lids heavy over her beautiful brown eyes. As she'd been when he'd woken her to make love.

'Don't hang up,' he said. 'It's me. Danny's in trouble and I need you to help me.'

He heard her shifting. Probably sitting up in bed. Out here on the cool night street he could feel how warm the sheets would be from her body. 'What's he done?'

'Silly bugger stole a car.'

She hissed in a sharp breath. 'Where is he?'

'Probably on the way to the police station by now.' He saw a cab and raised his hand to hail it. 'I'll be at yours to pick you up in ten minutes.'

'I'll call his parents. How do you know about this?'

'He rang me. He was in the back of the car.'

There was a long silence. 'Okay. I'll see you soon,' she said, quietly, and then ended the call.

As he climbed into the cab he wondered what that silence had meant.

Recriminations, tears, forms and a waiting room that held a hundred posters to instruct and a single dog-eared magazine. In the early morning light Elisabeth watched Danny and his parents get into a car and felt Angus standing beside her on the pavement.

He'd been serious. Magnificent. Supportive. Patient with Danny's parents. He'd helped her talk down Danny's father, who'd been ready to explode with rage, and tempered his condemnation of Danny's stupid actions with praise for the talent he'd seen in the boy and with an offer that had made the Williamses' mouths drop open.

After they'd all heard the details of Danny's arrest and what punishment a juvenile could expect with a guilty plea, the boy had been released into his parents' custody pending his appearance before a magistrate.

But when he'd appeared in the room, he'd gone straight to Angus.

'I'm sorry,' Danny said to Angus, his eyes shifting sideways to take Elisabeth and his parents into the apology.

Angus stepped aside so that Danny was facing his parents. 'Say that to your mum and dad.'

There were tears in the boy's eyes; Elisabeth thought that he looked as he must have as a small child, before he'd learned to hide his fear under anger and defiance.

'I'm sorry,' he said to his mother. 'I'm not going to do it again.'

Mrs Williams took him in her arms.

Elisabeth noticed that Angus had looked away. But not before she saw his face. He looked as he must have when he was younger, before he'd learned to hide his yearning under self-confidence.

And he hadn't had to be there in the first place. He hadn't needed to bring Elisabeth, either. He'd come because Danny needed him, and he'd known Elisabeth would want to help.

Elisabeth loved him so much she could barely stand it.

As the Williams family drove away the pinkness in the sky above the buildings was starting to fade. It was going to be a warm day. 'What time is it?' she asked. 'Around six?'

'Quarter to. We've got about four hours until the competition.'

'And only one competitor, now,' she said sadly.

She wanted Angus to put his arm around her shoulders. 'Should we walk for a little while?' he said instead. 'I could do with clearing my head.'

She nodded and they started down the street. She wasn't familiar with this part of London; she felt as if she were in a whole new city, a new world.

'Are you really going to let Danny apprentice at Magnum when he leaves school next year?' she asked.

'Yes. If I say I'll do something, I will. I keep trying to tell you that, Elisabeth.'

His face, when she glanced at it, was grim. His eyes looked tired. She flushed with shame at her words.

'I know,' she said. 'I know you will. I was just—it's a big risk for you.'

'Everything worthwhile is a risk. He'll start at the bottom and if he's good he'll work his way up.' Angus ran his hand through his dark hair and sighed. 'I owe him a lot.'

Elisabeth looked at him in surprise. 'You owe *him?*'

'I owe all three of you. You've shown me how much I can care. That there's more to me than the surface. But I owe Danny especially.'

'Why?'

'Because he's let me learn from his stupid mistakes. When he rang me he told me he'd helped steal the car because his mates wanted to and he didn't dare say no. He wanted acceptance at any price. He'd rather do something he knew was wrong than risk rejection. I don't want to be like that any more.'

She knew already that Angus had changed. She hadn't known she'd been one of the causes of it. She touched his arm briefly. 'I understand.'

'I don't quite think you do.' He stopped walking, and Elisabeth, confused, stopped too and faced him.

'Elisabeth, I love you,' he said.

The words made her step back, all the wind knocked out of her. She felt something hit the back of her thighs, and, without checking what it was, she sat on it before her legs collapsed beneath her.

'You do?'

'Yes. I do.' He smiled, brightening the whole world for a moment. 'You should see your face. You look absolutely tragic.'

'I wasn't expecting—'

'I know.' He sat down beside her on the low brick wall. 'The irony is, your reaction is exactly what I was expecting. That's why I haven't told you up till now.'

He was still smiling but the brilliance had gone. His face looked sad, his eyes heavy. Dark stubble shadowed his jaw and the dimple in his chin.

Pain sliced at her and she looked away at the street they'd been walking up, searching for a hint, a sign, a familiar landmark that would tell her what to do. How to stop them both hurting.

No luck. She was way, way beyond anywhere she had ever been before.

'We could be happy together,' he said. 'I know we would. We could get married and stick two fingers up at the gossipmongers and the press and it would be very good, Elisabeth.' He curled his magician's fingers around her hand, as if with his touch he could make everything he was saying come true. 'I love you so much.'

'You're not saying this to be noble? Because I might be pregnant?'

He barked out a laugh. 'Forget noble. I'm begging you, if you haven't noticed. This past week has been torture. I want to touch you, hold you, sleep with you, be with you in every way and all I've had is the Elisabeth with her walls up. If you're pregnant, that's great. But it's you that I want.'

'I…' She couldn't think when he was touching her, so she lifted her hand away from his. 'I can't.'

'You think you can't. But, Elisabeth, be a student for once. Learn from Danny. Don't throw away a chance of happiness because it's easier to do the wrong thing.'

She stood. Her ears were roaring, her hands shaking. 'It's not easy at all,' she choked. 'You say it's been torture for you—it's been hell for me. Every second, fighting and fighting what my body wants to do and I can't take it any more.'

He stood beside her and held out his arms to her. 'Stop fighting. Be with me. Even if you don't love me. Give in.'

*Even if you don't love me.* He didn't know the half of it, had no idea how close she was to losing herself entirely to him. She shook her head. 'No. I can't.'

He dropped his arms. 'You mean you won't.'

'The difference is only in words, Angus.' She looked around, anywhere except at him, and saw for the first time an underground station far down a side street and knew exactly where she was.

'I'm going to go home and get changed,' she said. 'I'll see you at ten.'

She turned and walked rapidly away from him, feeling the weight of his eyes on her back the entire time, like a cord joining the two of them that she was stretching and stretching thinner and thinner until it broke.

Jennifer was nearly as white as her uniform.

'Not here?' she whispered.

Elisabeth put her arm around the girl's narrow shoulders. 'There was an emergency and he couldn't compete. It's all right, Jennifer. You've done this plenty of times. And Danny wouldn't be anywhere near you anyway.'

Jennifer looked around the massive room, full of contestants and their supporters. From here, near the door, the stand-alone cooking workspaces looked like tiny islands in a sea of people and space.

'But I'm—I expected him to be here.'

Her voice was full of dismay. Elisabeth bit her lip in sympathy. Routine, repetition, a clear framework: it all created security. The smallest disruption, even if it wasn't strictly relevant, could crush confidence.

'You are going to be absolutely fine,' she told Jennifer with a cheerfulness she was far from feeling. 'Come on, let's find your workspace and check everything.'

Angus had been standing beside them in silence, letting Elisabeth deal with Jennifer's fear, but now he stepped forward.

'You've got talent, Jennifer, and nothing can stop talent. Talk me through what you're going to do. The clock starts. What do you pick up first?'

'I'll st-start the pasta,' she stammered, her voice barely above a whisper. As they walked across the floor a light flashed at them. Elisabeth blinked, seeing bright spots.

A photographer. The tabloids, of course, getting the celebrity chef and the teacher and the child for the front of their newspaper. Jennifer stopped, frozen, her face a picture of panic.

'Pasta,' prompted Angus gently. 'What's the first step?'

He touched her lightly on the elbow, got her moving again towards the workspace. Elisabeth trailed behind and watched as Angus let her talk her way through her panic. He took it step by step and reminded her of her routine, rebuilt the framework with words. When they reached the workspace she was still pale, but looked marginally less like a rabbit in headlights.

Marginally.

A woman with a clipboard approached Jennifer and started talking with her about the rules of the contest, how she'd be judged and what she wasn't allowed to do. Jennifer answered her in mumbled monosyllables.

Angus joined Elisabeth. He'd showered and shaved since she'd seen him, and wore a casual jacket and jeans that looked as elegant on him as a suit. She could smell his lemony scent, the freshness of his clothes and his skin, but his eyes still looked weary.

'I hope she doesn't choke,' he murmured.

'The next two hours might determine the course of her entire life,' Elisabeth said. 'I can't blame her for being scared.'

'If she's too scared, she won't be able to do it. Cooking well requires flexibility and confidence. That's where Danny excelled.' He shook his head. 'On a good day, he could've won this easily. Jennifer's technical skills are better, but I'm worried.'

'You've done your best,' she said, wanting to give him the same sort of comfort he'd just given Jennifer.

He smiled sadly. 'My best doesn't seem to be good enough these days.'

'Contestants, please take your places and family and friends take your seats; the Kid Culinaire competition will begin in ten minutes.'

Elisabeth scooted behind the counter to give Jennifer a hug. 'I believe in you,' she whispered in the girl's ear. Jennifer's hands clutched on to Elisabeth as if she were about to fall.

'I don't know if I can do it,' she whispered.

'Remember what Angus said. Food is emotion. You're not doing this for yourself; you're doing this because you remember your mum.' She squeezed the girl one last time and let her go.

'Put your feelings into it and take it one step at a time. I'm very proud of you. So is your dad. Your mum would be too.'

Jennifer nodded. When Elisabeth looked back at her on her way to the stands, the girl looked like a castaway in her own private world of fear.

Jennifer's father was already in his seat, and Jo was sitting beside him, chatting about cars, though Mr Keeling didn't say much. He drove a van for a living and had taken the day off work to come to the competition; Elisabeth suspected Jo's persuasive skills had come into that. She sat beside Joanna, noticing the two empty seats reserved for Danny's parents on the other side of Mr Keeling.

Angus sat next to her. As he took his seat a camera flashed again. 'I understand why the paparazzi get punched,' he muttered.

It would feel so natural to lean into him. Instead, she picked up her programme and pretended to scrutinise it until the room silenced around her and the announcer declared the start of the competition.

Two hours of cooking, and then the judges would taste and assess the finished products. All of the contestants looked very small from here. Especially Jennifer, who was standing utterly still.

'She needs to get started,' she heard Angus saying beside her. 'If you do the first step, the other steps are easier. One follows another like logic. The hardest part is starting.'

Jennifer moved. She took out a bowl and began to prepare her ingredients.

Elisabeth sighed in relief.

'What's she cooking?' Jo asked, and Angus began to explain.

Elisabeth looked at Mr Keeling listening to Angus. He was a heavy-set man, with some of Jennifer's paleness, and he looked as tired as Angus did, though without the reserves of energy and strength she knew Angus had. Joanna had told her the man worked all hours, often leaving Jennifer on her own overnight. Elisabeth wondered how much he worked to make ends meet, and how much he worked to keep himself busy after the death of his wife.

While the contestants worked, an announcer with a microphone wandered through the room, asking the kids questions about themselves and what they were cooking. *Don't choose Jennifer,* Elisabeth willed him as the minutes dragged on. The girl had developed a rhythm, and if she had to speak she could lose it.

'Where's the Welsh tango dancer?' she whispered to Jo, to distract herself from the tension.

'He had a dance-off in Cardiff. Wanted me to come, but I told him you needed me more. I'll tell you what, the tango really does teach a man some hip movements.'

Elisabeth smiled. 'Sounds like an interesting man. I should meet him for real.'

'You've tamed Angus MacAllister,' Jo replied. 'He hasn't flirted with me once since he's seen you. If I weren't so happy for you, I'd hate you for depriving the world of a precious natural resource.'

That knife of pain again. She hadn't told Jo that her relationship with Angus was over. She'd barely seen her in the past week, and they'd had plenty of other things to talk about: Dewi, the press, what Elisabeth was missing at school, and, today, Danny's arrest. Angus had been too painful a subject to bring up. She'd sidestepped every mention.

Back to her old tricks, she thought grimly.

'Jennifer Keeling, from the Slater School.' The announcer's voice came over the PA loud and clear. 'Hi, Jennifer.'

The girl's answer was inaudible.

'You're the only student from Slater, I hear,' the announcer continued. 'Your friend had to drop out unexpectedly. How does it feel to be representing your school?'

The girl didn't answer. Elisabeth could see her face reddening; even from here she could see her movements becoming jerkier, less fluent. The announcer tried again.

'I think I can safely say that you're the most famous of our contestants today, after your photograph was printed in last weekend's newspapers. How does it feel to be taught by a celebrity chef?'

'Angus is wonderful.' Her voice was small, but every word was clear.

Elisabeth looked over at Angus. He was leaning forward and there was a smile on his face. Not the blinding one, not the mischievous one, not the arrogant one. Just a smile.

She sat on her hands to stop herself pulling him to her and kissing that smile of pride and pleasure.

The announcer moved on to fresh meat and Elisabeth let herself relax the tiniest amount. An iota of relief, when every fibre of her being was strung as tightly as a drum.

One of the kids was a show-off, playing games with his knife, tossing his ingredients around his frying pan like one of the chef-performers in a Japanese steakhouse Elisabeth had been to once. The announcer spent some time with him, trading jokes. Danny would have been jealous if he'd been here, Elisabeth thought. But at least Jennifer was getting a reprieve.

She felt Angus tensing beside her and heard his sharp intake of breath. Immediately she focused on Jennifer. From here, she couldn't see anything wrong.

'What is it?' she whispered to him.

'That damn velouté,' he answered in low tones. 'She's stirring it like a clockwork elephant and if she doesn't take it off the heat in the next few seconds it's going to curdle again.'

She chewed on her fingertip as she watched Jennifer, concentrating as hard as she could on what the girl was doing. *Don't go wrong,* she thought, trying to send all of her extra nervous energy to the sauce in Jennifer's pan.

The exact moment it curdled she saw it on Jennifer's face, and heard it in Angus's groan. The girl took the pan off the heat and stood with it, transfixed by dismay and indecision.

She couldn't take it any more. Elisabeth stood, and slipped by Angus into the aisle. His knees brushed the side of her leg as she went by, and she saw him looking at her with concern.

'Need fresh air,' she told him. She hurried to the back of the room, through the lobby, and out onto the street.

It was a warm day, as she'd predicted, muggy and close with the overcast heat of early July. She breathed in the outside air full of petrol fumes and the smell of warm concrete. As oppressive as it was, it was still easier than being inside.

She shouldn't be out here. She should be supporting Jennifer at this moment of crisis. What if the girl looked up and saw her gone?

And these were the last few moments she would ever spend with Angus. Even though she couldn't touch him, could barely speak to him, every one was precious, heart-wrenchingly intense. Her watch said there was a little less than half an hour left of the competition. Twenty-six minutes with Angus, and then however long it took to judge, and then goodbye for ever.

Unless she was carrying his baby.

It was Saturday; she should have started her period on Thursday. She'd been late before. Stress could cause it, or not sleeping enough, and God knew she'd had plenty of both of those in the past week.

If they were having a baby, he'd sworn he'd stay with her. He'd offered to marry her. And not, he'd said, because he was being noble. Because he wanted her more than anything, because he loved her.

She spotted a chemist's shop down the street and she started for it. The suspense was too much to take. She'd find out, today, what the rest of her life held in store.

The inside of the shop was a bit cooler than outside. She found a blue box on the shelf. The last time she'd bought one of these tests it had been two and a half years ago and she had been excited, hopeful, sure the future was going to be bright.

The woman who rang up her purchase was in her fifties, very slim, with cat's-eye glasses and bouffant hair. 'I hope this turns out the way you want it to, dear,' she said. Elisabeth felt the woman's gaze on her left hand, where her third finger was conspicuously ringless.

And how did she want this to turn out? she thought as she left the shop, hid the test in her bag, and headed back for the building where the competition was being held.

If she was pregnant, she wouldn't have a choice. Her future would be mapped out for her in an instant. She would be with Angus; she would marry him. They would live together and bring up their child.

She bit back a sharp cry of longing.

And if she wasn't…

That would be it. She would thank Angus and leave him and she would continue on with the life she could understand.

In about an hour.

She threaded her way quietly back to the row of seats where she'd left Angus and Joanna and Mr Keeling. She looked for Jennifer and saw her chopping away furiously at something.

'She's done it,' Angus whispered to her as she passed him to get to her seat. 'She ditched the velouté and she's started something new. It looks like some sort of salsa with tarragon. She's improvising like I've never seen her do before. Brilliant.'

He was beaming, and Jo and Mr Keeling were practically on the edge of their seats. Elisabeth slid her bag under her chair.

His long body was folded into the chair beside her. His thigh was close to hers. She remembered Chanticleer, where she'd felt his knee under the table like an electric field, where he'd warmed the very air.

She knew every muscle of his body, every hair and every place that the bones were visible underneath his skin. She couldn't imagine knowing somebody else so intimately. Or opening herself to anyone else. He'd taken her apart and put her back together, overwhelmed her so much with pleasure that she'd laughed, helpless in his hands.

And what would their child look like? Dark hair, grey or brown eyes? Tall, surely, but with a dimple in the chin? Would it be a doer or a reader, a charmer or a teacher? Or something entirely new?

The minutes ticked by. She heard Angus and Joanna and Mr Keeling talking around her, and at times she replied, but she didn't know what they were saying. Instead she was trying to get up the courage to go to the ladies' room and take the pregnancy test.

Then the announcer said that time was up and the judging would begin and Elisabeth wondered frantically where those twenty-six minutes had gone, how they'd passed without her really appreciating them. They'd never come again. And it was too late to go do the test because now Jennifer had finished cooking and she was standing looking at them for support.

The judges went from student to student, tasting their dishes and dissecting them. They wrote comments on their clipboards.

'Jennifer's got a more ambitious menu than most of the other students,' Angus told them, 'but I'm not sure what view the judges will take of her modifying it because of her saucing disaster. She's presented it beautifully, though.'

'Do you think she'll win?' Elisabeth asked him.

He raised his shoulders. 'She's in the top five, I'd say. But I can't taste it, and that's what counts.'

It took a long time for the judges to make their way around the room, and then they huddled around a table to confer. Jennifer was exhausted, Elisabeth could tell; her thin face was pale and she leaned against the counter, watching the judges, while some of the other contestants talked with each other.

Elisabeth couldn't make her win. She couldn't even make her own life easier. She dug her fingers so tight into her thighs that they hurt and she wanted to stand up and scream.

Finally the lead judge took the microphone and, after a speech thanking all the contestants and their teachers and recounting some of the highlights of the day—a speech that was both necessary and right, Elisabeth knew, but which sounded in her ears like fingernails down an old-fashioned blackboard—he cleared his throat and started to announce the winners and to comment on their menus.

Second runner-up was a girl from Hackney, who'd made an Indian meal. 'Danny's was better,' Angus said to Elisabeth conspiratorially. She smiled, her heart sinking, at his loyalty.

First runner-up was a boy from Tooting. Angus's face was stormy. 'They've chosen him on the strength of his pasta; I'm not sure they'll choose a winning menu that features the same technique,' he muttered.

The judge paused and let the applause die away before he announced the winner. Elisabeth watched Jennifer. The girl was so alone down there. She'd barely been able to face her schoolmates and her teachers, the simplest things like raising her hand to speak in class, and now she was facing a moment that would tell her whether she'd succeeded or failed.

Jennifer lifted her chin. She straightened her spine. She turned her eyes, full and brave, on the judge.

The movements were subtle, unremarkable to anybody who didn't know Jennifer. Elisabeth drew in a breath of admiration.

Even if she didn't win, she was going to be okay. Elisabeth could see that Jennifer had made that decision.

'We debated about the winner,' the judge said. 'Though the quality of her work was clear, some of us were uncertain whether she should win. However, we all agreed that she put every ounce of her effort into her cooking, and when she failed she created something new with a creativity that cannot be taught, no matter who the teacher is.'

Elisabeth barely heard the rest, because Angus had thrown his arm around her and hugged her tight to his side and he was whispering, 'Yes!' through his broad smile, and it was too many good things at once. All she could understand through the confusion in her own head and heart were the words, 'First place, Jennifer Keeling.'

'Yes!' Angus roared. Jennifer turned to the audience and as the applause washed over the girl Elisabeth saw that she was smiling, bright and wide, straight at her father.

It was exactly what Elisabeth had wanted to happen, what she and Angus and Jennifer had worked so hard for over the past weeks. Jennifer had found her bravery and proved herself.

And Elisabeth felt numb.

It could be the last moment.

Mr Keeling burst across the row of seats and ran down the aisle to his daughter to take her in his arms. Jo was jumping up and down cheering and hooting. They didn't need her right now.

She had to know, and then she could feel.

'Sorry,' she said to Angus, and slipped under his arm and into the aisle without meeting his eye. Quickly she went to the back of the room and found the Ladies'.

Her fingers could barely lock the cubicle after her and it took several fumbling attempts before she got the Cellophane off the box and the pregnancy test in her hand. She followed the instructions and then stood, her hand shaking, in the cubicle waiting for the result in the window.

When the window began to colour in blue, she was no less numb than she had been before.

Slowly, she slid the bolt on the door and opened it and stepped out.

Angus stood before her. His dark hair and jacket stood out in the gleaming white room; he looked too big for the small sinks, the women's lighted mirrors, but he was the first thing on her mind and it seemed natural he should be there.

'What's wrong?' he asked, his gravelly voice echoing off the tiles.

She couldn't speak. She handed him the test.

He squinted down at it. 'What does this mean?'

'A blue line means you're not pregnant. A blue cross means you are.'

Angus gazed down at the bright blue line. And then he looked at her, and his face was such a picture of her own emotions that she suddenly wasn't numb any more.

The tears came out of deep inside her without warning. She stepped forward and straight into his arms.

He enfolded her. Her safe forest, her most beautiful dream. He held her and rocked her and she cried deep racking sobs that she could control no more than the wind.

'Elisabeth,' he whispered to her. 'Darling, sweet Elisabeth. It will happen. You will have a baby, please God with me, but you will. Everything will be fine. I promise you.'

'I wanted,' she gasped, and couldn't finish.

It was too much loss, all at once. This hope, the thought of her baby lost beforehand and the tears that had never come, not in two years. It was all the pain she had been so afraid of. Everything she had fought and fought against, and she was feeling it anyway.

Her walls had never helped her after all.

And Angus was holding her, kissing the top of her head. Promising everything would be all right.

She leaned against him, heard his heart beating and felt the cloth of his shirt wet against her cheek. She thought of the teenager she'd just watched facing her worst fears and winning.

*Be here now and for ever.*

'I wanted a baby,' she said. 'With you.' She tightened her arms around him and lifted her chin. His face was blurred with her tears and his own eyes were bright and wet. 'I love you.'

He sucked in a breath. And stared at her. 'You mean it.'

Something in his face made her start to smile. 'Yes.'

'Say it again.'

'I love you.'

A tear spilled down his cheek and it was blinding, brilliant, beautiful.

'And you'll stay with me,' he said. 'Please.'

The choice had seemed so difficult before, and now it was so easy. She could put herself in his hands, because he was in her hands, too.

'I want to be with you for ever,' she said.

He kissed her and she had never realised how perfect a kiss could be.

'We'll get married,' he murmured against her lips, 'and then we'll try for a family together. That's the order you want to do it in, isn't it?'

She kissed him and she wiped her eyes. 'Actually,' she said, 'it's the trust that matters. Not the wedding ring.'

'But we'll get married anyway.'

The door to the ladies' room opened, letting in some of the noise of the crowd beyond it.

'Oh, goodness, I am sorry,' a voice said, and Elisabeth and Angus glanced over to see a brown coat and high-heeled shoes retreating.

Angus cleared his throat. 'I forgot this was the Ladies'.'

Elisabeth couldn't help giggling.

'Angus, do you realise that our first kiss was in a refrigerator and you've just proposed to me in a toilet?'

His eyes glinted with mischief. 'Are you implying that I'm acting in bad taste? Do you want me to get down on my knees and ask you if you'll marry me?'

'No,' she laughed, and then realised she didn't know which question she had answered. 'I mean yes—I mean no, don't get down on your knees.'

'Just say yes. It's less grammatically complicated.'

'Yes.'

She felt a funny tickling in her stomach. Not like the tension sickness she'd felt earlier, or the butterflies she'd had through the judging. More like the sparkling bubbles of champagne. A glorious intoxication, thrilling, unpredictable, and precious. The two of them together could face down any fear.

She kissed him, full of promise and embracing the uncertainty. More delicious than any other pleasure.

He pulled her up against him and trailed his hands up and down her body.

'What do we do next?' he murmured.

'Later, tomorrow, we tell everybody in the world. And then we spend the rest of our lives making love.' She straightened his collar, brushed back his hair, felt so right touching him. 'But now, let's go help Jennifer celebrate.'

# EPILOGUE

'ALL ready,' Angus said.

Before she put her book down on the crocheted afghan that covered the back of her favourite chair, Elisabeth reread two lines in preparation for tomorrow's lesson.

*But my true love is grown to such excess*
*I cannot sum up sum of half my wealth.*

Shakespeare said it better than she ever could. She smiled, stood, straightened her dress, and went into the kitchen after Angus.

He'd set the table with candles and fresh flowers, but they were no match for him, tall and sexy in tailored trousers, a blue shirt rolled up to expose his muscular forearms and dextrous wrists and hands. She knew every scar, every mark, every moment of his life.

Angus pulled out a chair for her and dropped a kiss on her head when she sat down.

The plate in front of her was a work of art. She heard the pop of a bottle of champagne and when he leaned over her to pour her a glass she breathed in his scent, more seductive than the aroma of the food he'd cooked.

'Is this something new?' she asked.

He grinned. 'Danny designed the menu in our honour and taught me how to make it. He's been experimenting at Magnum all week.'

'The apprentice is teaching the master, huh?'

'I learn something new every day. At work and at home.'

'And you're going to have to learn how to cook vegan meals

when my parents get here for their visit. My father hasn't eaten meat since nineteen sixty-one.'

'Not a problem. I learn quickly, as you know. For example, I knew I was going to fall in love with you from the first moment I saw you terrorising my chicken.'

Elisabeth threw back her head and laughed in delight at the pure, magic wonder of Angus MacAllister. She lifted her champagne glass.

'Happy first anniversary,' she said.

'Happy first anniversary, Mrs MacAllister.' They chimed glasses and leaned over the table to share a lingering, tender kiss.

'The food looks delicious,' Elisabeth breathed. 'But aren't you forgetting something?'

'What's that, love?'

'Your son can't use a fork yet.'

They both looked at their dark-haired, brown-eyed, dimple-chinned son, gurgling happily in his high chair, and waving his hands at the meticulously presented dish of food in front of him.

'It's never too early to appreciate good plating. Isn't that right, Ewan, mate?'

Angus kissed his son on his cheek and picked up his plate. He took it to the worktop and scraped the contents into the food processor.

'We can't have him thinking that all food is mushy and comes in bowls, can we?' he called over the noise of the machine.

'For him, it pretty much does.'

Elisabeth accepted the bowl of processed food from Angus and spooned a bit into Ewan's mouth. The little boy held his mouth open for more.

'See, he likes it. He's got good taste. I think he's going to be a chef like his old man.' Angus leaned over the table and ruffled Ewan's fine hair.

'At the moment, he's more interested in becoming a nudist like his grandparents.'

'There are definite benefits to being nude,' Angus commented, sitting back in his chair. 'I'll show you some of them after his bedtime.'

Elisabeth fed Ewan another spoonful and glanced at her husband's face. Angus was regarding them both with an expression of pleasure and pride. Exactly the way she felt.

'Yes, Chef,' she said, and watched his smile broaden.

A tiny grunt brought her attention back to their baby. Ewan screwed up his face, pursed his lips, and blew. A splatter of processed food sailed across the room and landed squarely in Angus's champagne glass.

Elisabeth felt the smile grow on her own face.

'Bad news,' she told Angus. 'I think he's going to grow up to be a critic.'

Chosen by him for business,
taken by him for pleasure…
A classic collection of office romances from
Harlequin Presents, by your favorite authors.

*Coming in September:*

# THE BRAZILIAN BOSS'S INNOCENT MISTRESS
## by Sarah Morgan

Innocent Grace Thacker has ten minutes to persuade
ruthless Brazilian Rafael Cordeiro to help her.
Ten minutes to decide whether to leave and lose—
or settle her debts in his bed!

*Also from this miniseries, coming in October:*

# THE BOSS'S WIFE FOR A WEEK
## by Anne McAllister

HP12664

# REQUEST YOUR FREE BOOKS!

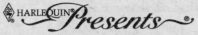 HARLEQUIN® *Presents~*

## 2 FREE NOVELS
## PLUS 2
## FREE GIFTS!

---

**YES!** Please send me 2 FREE Harlequin Presents® novels and my 2 FREE gifts. After receiving them, if I don't wish to receive any more books, I can return the shipping statement marked "cancel." If I don't cancel, I will receive 6 brand-new novels every month and be billed just $3.80 per book in the U.S., or $4.47 per book in Canada, plus 25¢ shipping and handling per book and applicable taxes, if any*. That's a savings of close to 15% off the cover price! I understand that accepting the 2 free books and gifts places me under no obligation to buy anything. I can always return a shipment and cancel at any time. Even if I never buy another book from Harlequin, the two free books and gifts are mine to keep forever.

106 HDN EEXK  306 HDN EEXV

Name _____ (PLEASE PRINT)

Address _____ Apt. #

City _____ State/Prov. _____ Zip/Postal Code

Signature (if under 18, a parent or guardian must sign)

Mail to the **Harlequin Reader Service®**:
**IN U.S.A.:** P.O. Box 1867, Buffalo, NY 14240-1867
**IN CANADA:** P.O. Box 609, Fort Erie, Ontario L2A 5X3

Not valid to current Harlequin Presents subscribers.

**Want to try two free books from another line?**
**Call 1-800-873-8635 or visit www.morefreebooks.com.**

\* Terms and prices subject to change without notice. NY residents add applicable sales tax. Canadian residents will be charged applicable provincial taxes and GST. This offer is limited to one order per household. All orders subject to approval. Credit or debit balances in a customer's account(s) may be offset by any other outstanding balance owed by or to the customer. Please allow 4 to 6 weeks for delivery.

**Your Privacy:** Harlequin is committed to protecting your privacy. Our Privacy Policy is available online at www.eHarlequin.com or upon request from the Reader Service. From time to time we make our lists of customers available to reputable firms who may have a product or service of interest to you. If you would prefer we not share your name and address, please check here. ☐

HP07

# HARLEQUIN *Presents*